LOW KEY FALLIN' FOR A SAVAGE 2

J. DOMINIQUE

Cole Hart
SIGNATURE SERIES

Low Key Fallin' For A Savage 2

Copyright © 2020 by J. Dominique

All rights reserved.

Published in the United States of America.

Published by Cole Hart Signature, LLC.

Mailing List

To stay up to date on new releases, plus get information on contests, sneak peeks, and more,

Go To The Website Below...

www.colehartsignature.com

TEXT TO JOIN

To stay up to date on new releases, plus get exclusive information on contests, sneak peeks, and more...

Text ColeHartSig to (855)231-5230

PREVIOUSLY...

DREAM

I'd thought about the idea of visiting Budda for almost a week before finally making a decision. I was sure that to Destiny, it seemed like my mind was made up, but really I had been going back and forth about it. Opening myself up to him was some scary and stupid shit, I can admit that. However, me not going and confronting him though was even more frightening. My subtle hints had been going ignored, so it was safe to assume that his crazy ass still had hope. I was going so that I could squash that hope, and maybe keep my man from doing something stupid.

To keep Elijah in the dark, I'd told him I would be working all day and told everybody at the salon that I would be with him. It was very tv sitcom-ish, but I was hoping it would work for me. Elijah should've been in meetings all day anyway. He also had a club opening and was remodeling a closed down YMCA so that he could start up his mentorship program.

So I had a small window to get this done and be in and out. I kept telling myself that this should be easy once I got checked in, but I couldn't stop myself from shaking, and it wasn't from the cold. My nerves were at in all time high. In just one week Illinois had started acting like a bitch, so instead of the sundress and jean jacket I thought

I was going to wear, I was stuck in a pair of blue jeggings that had my ass looking plump! My top was a plain white bodysuit that had a mock turtle neck. Every man in the building had their eyes on me, and I can't say I blamed them. I was here to make Budda cry from how fine I was.

As soon as I walked into the visiting room, Budda laid eyes on me, and a wide grin covered his face, with his eyes lit up. I dodged his extended arms and took a seat at the table with a hard stare. Amused, he smirked and took a seat across the table from me, eating me up with his dark eyes.

"Damn, you look good!" He gushed.

"What do you want Brian?"

His brows shot up like he was shocked by my demeanor. "Straight to the point, huh?" He chuckled leaning onto the table. I didn't even bother to answer him. I just crossed my arms over my chest and tilted my head.

"Okay, okay. You already know I want us to be together. I told you a nigga was getting out soon so I'm tryna see if we can start over." This nigga had the nerve to smile like he was offering me a big prize or something.

"Oh, really? Should I just forget about all the hell you put me through? All the hoes and mind games?" I hissed. "Keeping me prisoner to that damn house or tracking my every move! How about when you tried to make me take the wrap for those fucking drugs, huh? I don't want to live like that any more- I won't live like that ever again!"

"What you want me to say, Shay? I told you a million times I'm sorry! That shit was years ago! I'm different now-."

"Oh, you different now?" I mocked him with my lips turned up. "Let me guess.... You found God while you were in here? That's what you said last time, you know, right before you were going to get out and let's not forget the time when you stomped my baby out of me." I shouted as I moved into his line of vision since he was avoiding eye contact. I hadn't told anyone about some of the fucked up things that he'd done and some stuff I suppressed just because it hurt too bad.

He glared my way angrily. "Don't fuckin test me like I won't fuck you up in here Dream!"

"You know what, fuck you! I only came up here to let you know that I'm not comin' back to you! I'm happy! I have a man who treats me like a queen, and he loves the ground I walk on. So when you get out, if you get out, do not come anywhere near me. We're more than done!"

"Oh, so you gave my pussy away and thought that's gonna be it?" He swiped his nose, which usually meant he was mad as hell. The fact that we were in a highly secure prison was the only reason that move alone didn't have me shaking in my UGGs. Instead, I took great pleasure in knowing that if he even jumped the tall ass guards in the corner would take his ass down.

"Out of everything I just said that's all you heard?"

"I heard all that shit." He waved me off. "I'm even willing to forgive you because no matter what you sayin', I know Eazy ain't fuckin you like me." I was so caught off guard by him mentioning Eazy that my mouth fell open, but no words would come out.

"Wh-wha?"

"Oh, you thought that nigga really wanted you?" Now it was his turn to smirk as he sized me up. I flinched away from his touch when he tried to caress my face. "It's cool, Shay. I'm really not that mad. I mean he wasn't supposed to fuck you, just keep an eye on you, but that's what I been saying since the beginning. You're too naïve to be out here alone without me. You can't even think for yourself."

The look on his face gave me chills, and for some reason, I couldn't help but wonder if what he said was true. Could Elijah have been playing me this whole time? Was all this shit just a game for him? As these questions floated around my head, the guards yelled out that the visit was over. I hadn't even planned on staying that long, but I was damn sure ready to go. And even though I was questioning Elijah on the inside, I wouldn't let Budda know he'd gotten to me. If I knew for sure I wouldn't be at risk for catching a charge, I would've spit right in his face, but instead, I stood over him as he sat perfectly still, pleased with himself.

"Fuck you Budda!" I walked away quickly so that he couldn't see the tears in my eyes.

"You're mine, Shay! I don't care what you think, you gon always be my bitch!" He yelled at my back as I hurried out. Of course, now everybody was looking at this crazy ass nigga and me, further embarrassing me just like always. I damn sure should have listened when Destiny told me not to come because once again Budda had gotten the upper hand and I didn't feel any better. If anything I felt worse and even more paranoid than I'd been before visiting. The most fucked up part about the whole thing was that he had managed to tear down everything Elijah and I had built in a matter of minutes.

Eazy

I had been running around ever since I climbed out of Dream's bed that morning. After meeting with a few investors about the mentorship program, I shot over to check on the status of my nightclub and then to my house to see how much progress they'd made on the damage Sherice had caused. Just like last time they got to running their mouths about it being another six months. The street nigga in me was ready to threaten their asses, but my business head prevailed and merely advised them that they'd better adjust that shit or they'd be out of a job.

By lunch I was ready to call it a day, but there was other shit I had to take care of. Not only did I need to holla at our lawyer, but I also had to stop by and talk to Juice. The shit with Budda still had me fucked up. I was walking around like everything was good, but in reality, finding out that my nigga and mentor was on some snake shit had me looking at everybody suspect as fuck. I came up under the principles that Budda had taught me. My whole business was set up according to the advice he'd given me. No matter what, don't snitch! Treat your workers fair! Never turn your back on your day ones. I'd lived and breathed that shit, and the whole time his ass was fraud.

Since Trell had come to me with this shit, I had been working over-time to make sure our shit was straight and that we weren't on the Feds or nobody else's radar. So far nothing had come up, but I was close to just going ahead and shutting shit down until I figured out what I was going to do about Budda. I hated to say it, but I was leaning towards Juice's method of just putting that nigga out of his misery. First, I had to find out what all he was involved in though. For all I knew we were reading too much into the shit and had nothing to worry about, but all my years in the streets taught me to trust my instincts and my instincts were saying that shit was about to get real hectic.

My phone went off letting me know my mama was calling, and I took my time sliding the bar across the screen. I wasn't in the best mood, and if anybody would be able to tell, it would be Rachel King.

"Hey ma," I answered, trying to sound as normal as possible.

"Hey, baby! How's your day going?" She gushed, and I could hear the sounds of the shop in the background, letting me know she was at work.

I unbuttoned the jacket on my Tom Ford suit and reclined my seat getting comfortable. "It's going good so far, I guess. Just tryna light a fire under these niggas to finish my house. How you doing, though? Y'all up in there snatching edges and shit?"

"Elijah I don't know who's worse, you or Jeremiah with that fuckin cussin'." She laughed.

"I wonder where we get it from?"

"Oh, see you tried it! You ain't gone blame that shit on me! Y'all got that shit from EJ." Shaking my head at her lying ass, I brushed my hand down my waves and chuckled.

"I'm tellin pops you over there lyin' on him and shit."

"Boy bye! That nigga knows how foul his mouth is. Anyway." She huffed, and I could imagine her rolling her eyes. "I don't wanna mess up you and Dream's plans, but I forgot your father has a doctor's appointment and I need her to come in for maybe an hour or two. Destiny's here, but we're swamped today."

"Dream?" My grip on the phone tightened, and I pinched the bridge of my nose.

"Yes, nigga Dream! I tried calling her, but the phone kept going to voicemail."

"Dream told you she was gone be with me?" I had to clarify just to make sure I wasn't tweaking. Fucking around with Budda I didn't know what was what these days, so before I started tearing shit up I needed to be positive I understood her right.

"Oh shit." She grumbled under her breath, and I knew my assumptions were accurate. Dream had told me that she was going to be working all day, she said that she was booked up until they closed. I squeezed my eyes shut and tried to alleviate the tension I felt in my forehead. I don't need this shit right now! Another call came through as my mama tried to explain away Dream's lies, and I rushed her off the phone, not even caring. I wasn't trying to hear that shit from her. There was no need for Dream to lie to me about her whereabouts unless she was on some sneaky shit! I wasn't trying to be fucking with another lying ass female. Clicking over I saw that it was Trell calling.

"What's up bruh?"

"Aye, you ain't gone believe this shit my nigga, come over to my spot." He said quickly before hanging up. I'd put him on to find out as much as he could about the Budda situation since I didn't trust anybody else to do this shit. If he was calling and couldn't say shit over the phone, then that meant that he'd found something. I straightened up and sped out of the parking lot as questions about Dream and Budda fought for attention in my head. Both situations were serious and would need to be addressed as soon as possible, but at the moment, I needed to deal with the most dangerous one first.

Dream could be just as shady as Sherice, and as much as I loved her, I knew how to walk away from shit that didn't mean me any good. Budda though, he was an entirely different story. He could fuck with my money and my freedom so that would take precedence.

I made it to Trell's crib in less than an hour and barely put the car in park trying to get out. He met me at the door with a grim look on his face holding a Manila envelope.

"Come on in."

I ducked inside, aware of how crazy I probably looked sweating and out of breath. As he led the way into his kitchen, I loosened my tie and tried to get my breathing under control. He set the folder down on top of the island and leaned over it.

"You look like shit nigga, the fuck going on?" He asked, finally taking in my appearance with concern.

I shook my head because I didn't want to bring Dream up and distract from the matter at hand. "I'm cool. Just gon' head show me what you found." His face displayed unease, and he hesitated briefly before flipping open the folder.

"This is the original police report from the night Budda got knocked." Trell pointed to the first sheet of paper. I skimmed through quickly reading about how he'd gotten pulled over for swerving. It noted that he was in the car with a female and since Budda's dumb ass was acting irate and the passenger appeared to show signs of being beaten up they put him in cuffs and searched the car. In disbelief, I read how they found two kilos of cocaine in the trunk, and he immediately told them it wasn't his' it was the girls'. The shit that threw me for a loop though out of everything on there was Dream's name as clear as day. I released a breath I hadn't realized I'd been holding and looked at Trell who just nodded for me to keep going so I did.

After not being able to pin the drugs on Dream, Budda cut a deal with the state to give up his team for a lighter sentence and to have his records sealed on the condition that he give up his connect and any associates upon his release. This nigga had turned on everybody, and while we all thought his guys had fallen off and just ducked out the game, he had gotten them all arrested. I flipped through the paperwork getting more and more pissed off by the second. Especially knowing that Dream had dealings with this nigga. Had she scoped me out for him? Was she fraud this whole time? I smacked the entire stack of papers off the desk and started ramming my fists into Trell's stainless steel refrigerator until they were bleeding. Fuck what I'd said about waiting! As soon as that nigga touched down, he was dead!

"You done hulk cause that ain't it?" Trell asked once I'd stopped and was standing there breathing heavily. So far, the only thing that I was holding on to was the fact that my name hadn't been mentioned yet. As much as I would've wanted to believe that it was because Budda fucked with me I knew it was a reason and not one that benefited me.

"Gone head man!" I snapped waiting for him to drop another bomb.

"Ayite so after seeing all that shit, I figured I should check and see who been visiting that nigga. You know just because he's getting out soon and shit." He hesitated again.

"Gone head nigga spit it out!"

"Well twelve ain't been up there, but yo girl Dream went to see him today."

JUICE

I pulled up to Yo'Sahn's school to drop him off for practice. Real shit I couldn't wait to get his little ass up out my shit so I could go and snap on his damn mama. It had been some days since he told me about her talking to some nigga and I was ready to nip that shit in the bud. Call me selfish, but I wasn't ready for somebody else to come swooping in and take my woman. I'd have to work on some shit because I was still fucking Makalah, but I was willing to cut her ass off for Destiny. I didn't know if I would be willing to cut off bitches in the future, but at this moment I was prepared to.

He dapped me up and got out flossing in the latest J's. As usual, I waited to make sure he got into the building, but as soon as I saw Jayden's little nappy head ass stop him, I reached for my seatbelt. He was standing with a group of niggas, but I knew his face anywhere. Whatever he said to Yo'Sahn had him dropping his shit ready to fight, and I damn near ran over there.

"Get y'all lil asses back!" I barked stopping in front of them. They all froze up and looked my way like I was supposed to be scared or some shit. "Yo'Sahn you straight?"

He didn't answer me. He was so busy staring Jayden down with his fists balled up. "Take that shit back!"

I glanced back and forth between the two as Jayden grinned. "Make me pussy!"

"Fuck this lil nigga! Gone take yo ass to practice." I snatched his bag up and pushed it into his chest while simultaneously giving him a light shove towards the door.

"Yeah listen to yo step daddy and take yo ass on!"

"Aye, you really out here actin' like I give a fuck about you being ten nigga! Don't let these grown muhfuckas send you off! I'll let my mans beat yo ass and go to practice like ain't shit happened!" I was starting to get pissed off because I should've been gone already, but I wasn't about to leave Yo'Sahn out here by himself. It ain't take a rocket scientist to know that as soon as I peeled out, they'd try and jump him. Low key I felt like if Jayden got his ass beat real good, he might let go of this street shit, but I didn't want Yo'Sahn to have to be the one to do it. He had too much to lose while Jayden ain't have shit.

"Man fuck you!" He raised his middle fingers up at me and grabbed his little junk before running off with the rest of them clowns. When I caught his little ass, I was gone give him the ass whooping his daddy was supposed to. I made a mental note to start wearing my thickest leather belt from now on because I was sure to see him when I dropped Yo'Sahn off or picked him up. Grumbling I started towards my damn car only stopping because Yo'Sahn still hadn't gone inside.

"Them Lil niggas ain't on shit ayite gone head inside," I told him as he hesitated on the first step. He was just about to turn around and do what I said when the sound of screeching tires had us both looking towards the street where a black car was. All I saw was a flash before bullets started spraying our way. We were out in the open with nothing to cover us, so I jumped on top of Yo'Sahn and pulled out my gun. I stayed covering his body with mine as I emptied my clip into the moving vehicle. A second later you wouldn't even have been able to tell that some niggas had come through there blasting besides the thick smell of gun powder. The whole block was silent, or maybe it was the ringing in my ears that wasn't allowing me to hear shit. With pain soaring through my chest and arm, I went to turn Yo'Sahn over.

"Yo'Sahn, you straight! Aye! Yo'Sahn!" I shook him even as blood leaked from his mouth. "Yo-, Yo'Sahn!" My voice cracked, and my breathing became heavy. I was trying to fight through the pain, as a group of people ran towards us, but they were all blurry as hell, and I couldn't even make out what they were saying.

"Hold on young man. Stay with me!" That was the last thing I heard before everything faded to black.

MEANWHILE INSIDE THE BLACK CAR...

"Hell yeah! Did you see that shit!" I yelled excitedly as we sped through the streets, making our getaway. I was on a high right now! The only thing that would've been better was if I had gotten to see that nigga take his last breath.

"You said you was only gone shoot Juice nigga! You hit the fuckin kid too!" Grim whined like a little bitch.

"His ass was in the way! Fuck I look like not taking a clean shot cause that lil nigga was close! Yo ass sound stupid!" I lied just that quick. Yo'Sahn had been a pain in my ass since I met him. The way I saw it why not kill two birds with one stone. This shit was gone kill that bitch Destiny and I couldn't wait! It was about time them mutha-fuckas felt my pain. That bitch ain't give a fuck about Juice supposedly killing me, so I didn't give a fuck about taking out her little snot-nosed kid.

"Mannnn this shit ain't right!" His big ass huffed causing me to give him the side-eye. Besides him helping me get better after Juice shot me I didn't have no reason to trust him. After all, he'd only decided to help once I let him know that Juice and Eazy's reign was about to be over. When they closed the trunk on me, I for real thought my ass was dead, but I only passed out.

The second Grim opened the trunk to drop my ass in a ditch somewhere I let him know that Budda was my cousin and not only was he about to hand Juice and Eazy over to the Feds, but he was about to take over. It ain't take much more convincing than that.

I was the only nigga that Budda had left out of his paperwork, and that was only because our daddies were brothers. Of course when he went down, I tried to hustle on my own before finally going to Eazy. Without my cousin around I really wasn't shit though so of course I fell off, but that shit wasn't my fault. They should've known better! Did a background check or something, but since they didn't, they got hit. I knew that nigga Juice would kill me though, so I stole Destiny's money to pay them back and kept the rest for myself minus the couple hundreds I left in there. The fact that she wasn't regularly checking her money was dumb on her part.

It was obvious that her hoe ass was the reason Juice came up to the strip club on his bullshit, but what he wasn't expecting was for me to still be alive. Now his ass was the one dead or at least almost there. I'd put enough bullets in him to put 50 cent down, so I know his ass wasn't gone walk away.

"Just hit the corner and shut the fuck up!" I snapped angrily, and he did as he was told just like a good puppy. As soon as we hit the next street, I spotted the little nigga I was looking for and called him over.

"What's up!" Jayden panted out of breath once he made it to the car.

"Good lookin'," I said slipping him ten crispy hundred dollar bills. His face lit up at the sight of the money, and I had a mind to shoot his little ass too just in case he ended up talking, but instead, I tapped Grim so he could pull off. We had one more stop to make.

It took another hour to get to one of Budda's old warehouses, but the second we pulled in, and he put the car in park I sent a single bullet through the side of his head. I wasn't even moved by the amount of blood and brain matter that splashed on the window as I stepped out coolly and shut the door.

"Damn you had to kill his ass already?" Budda asked, coming from around the side of the building dressed in black.

"His ass was cryin' and shit bout Yo'Sahn. Besides how fast he turned on them niggas we ain't need his ass around no more." I shrugged.

"Facts." Budda agreed. "You ready to turn the city out?"

"Hell yeah!" Chicago wasn't gone never be the same after Dre and Budda took over.

To be continued ...

DREAM

I hadn't been able to sit still since I'd returned from my visit with Budda. Not only had he solidified his reach beyond the walls, but he'd ruined what I thought was a real relationship. A part of me wanted to believe that he was full of shit, and would be willing to say anything to fuck with me, but I knew better. Budda was the king of mind games and if messing with my mental was his goal, then he'd definitely accomplished it. Here I was with the best man I'd ever had, and now I was wondering if it was all a ploy. I paced the floor in my bedroom and sipped on a glass of wine trying to relax so that I could think clearly, but neither was working. Truthfully, I wanted to confront Elijah and curse his ass out! How dare he play with my emotions and to involve my nephew in this bull-shit! That thought was enough to make me polish off the remainder of my drink with my mind made up. Grabbing my phone and keys off the dresser, I headed out while dialing his number.

"Hey, baby, I thought you were gonna be busy today." He answered quickly. His tone was accusatory, but that could've just been my paranoia.

"Oh yeah well I got a little break and figured I'd come see you while I was out grabbing some food." The lie rolled off my tongue like I'd practiced it as I slid into my car and started it up.

"Ahhh you missed a nigga huh?"

"Is that a crime?" I asked sweetly with a roll of my eyes while he chuckled, probably thinking he had me wrapped around his fingers.

"Nah ain't nothing wrong with that at all. Slide through though; I'm at the crib."

"I'll be there in a minute then," I told him in a flat tone and disconnected the call. As mad as I was, my heart still pounded against my chest at the promise of being close to him. It was literally a war raging inside me as I headed towards his apartment. My mind was trying to tell me that Elijah was no good while my heart fought to believe in what we had. I cut the radio up as high as it would go to try and drown out my thoughts while driving the short distance to him. My playlist reflected the mood I'd been in lately filling my car with soft crooning about love and all that good shit, further influencing my thoughts.

Before I knew it, I was pulling into his driveway. I shut my car off but didn't get out right away because I needed a few seconds to get myself together before I saw him. My phone went off with a call from Destiny while I tried to get my emotions under control, and after sending the call to voicemail, I went ahead and shut it off. This was not a conversation that could be had with distractions. I wanted to look this nigga in his eyes and ask him if he'd spent this whole time lying to me for my ex even though I already knew the truth. Taking a deep breath, I stepped out and started up the walkway just as Elijah opened the door looking as handsome as ever. Dressed simply in red basketball shorts, a black t-shirt, black socks and Nike slides, he hit me with a lopsided grin that had a bittersweet effect. Once I was close enough, he pulled me inside and into a hug, hypnotizing me with his signature scent and kissing me deeply. It was like he knew exactly what he was doing because I was left unable to speak. Hell, I almost forgot what I even came over for in the first place.

"Damn, I guess I missed yo ass too." He said never removing his lips from mine. I had to admit that it felt good being in his arms, too good almost. "Did you wear this to work?"

His question brought me out of my haze, and I realized that I still had on the clothes I wore to the visit. Elijah knew better than anybody the dress code that I'd put in place since he saw me getting dressed most mornings, and the white bodysuit and blue jeggings were not work attire. He backed away just enough to take me in with a slight frown and questioning eyes.

"I…..I um."

"You what….? You bouta lie Dream?" He goaded suddenly glaring at me, and if I didn't know any better, I'd swear he knew exactly where I'd been.

"What-?" I answered lamely.

"I know you weren't at the shop today. You went to Statesville, right?" His question didn't require an answer. Judging from the murderous look on his face, it was obvious that he already knew. What I wanted to know was how he could stand there looking as if I'd betrayed him when he was in the wrong.

"Yeah, I went to see my ex, Budda, and he told me all about y'all little scheme too. You around here actin like I did something wrong when you're the one that's been on some fraud shit this whole time." My voice trembled as I finally let the effects of his betrayal show.

"Scheme?" He seemed genuinely confused, but I wasn't letting him off the hook so easy.

"Yes, scheme nigga! Did he pay you to find me and you just decided to get some pussy while you were at it? Huh?"

Even through my tear-filled gaze, I could see his face twist in a mix of anger and bewilderment, but I know it was all bull shit! I swear if his life of crime didn't work out, the nigga could damn sure take up acting. He could pretend all he wanted though, the fact that he knew where I was proved he'd been talking to Budda. How else would he have known?

"Why the fuck I always gotta get the crazy ones, bruh!" He grumbled to himself, shaking his head and chuckling bitterly. I was immediately offended by him putting me in the same category as Sherice, especially when I could say the same thing, but he cut me off before I could express my displeasure with the comparison. "Yeah, I know Budda's grimy ass from when I was comin up, and I been lookin' out for him his whole bid, but as far as plotting with him to get at you? Nah, that's bitch shit. What would I even gain from that Dream? You though? You lookin' real conniving right now." Suddenly, he pulled a big ass, silver gun from the waistband of his shorts and held it down by his side. "When I found out you were the Shay that Budda always talked about I wasn't even trippin' that hard, but then yo ass lied about work today just so that you could go visit that nigga? On the strength of Yo'Sahn I'm tryna give you the benefit of the doubt, so you better make this good. What is he planning?"

At this point I didn't know who this nigga was right now and that had me scared as hell. Instinctively, I'd taken a step back and damn near pissed myself when he'd first pulled the gun out, but the fact that he hadn't pointed it at me gave me some hope as I tried to digest everything he'd just said. Since he'd laid it all on the table I could see how Budda had twisted this situation and not only had I fallen for it, but I'd risked my relationship and now my life just for his amusement it seemed. I didn't know how to explain why after all of the hurt he'd caused me I would go and visit him. I could tell Elijah the truth, but that shit sounded stupid even as I said it in my head, so I knew he wasn't going to go for that.

He tilted his head impatiently while I continued to back away until there was nowhere left to go. Still, I pressed myself into the back of his couch like it would disappear and allow me more space to run. "I-." I didn't get a chance to finish whatever was about to come out of my mouth because his phone started going off. He took his sweet time removing it from his pocket to glance at the screen, before stuffing it back and returning his dark eyes to me.

Thankfully, whoever was trying to reach him wasn't letting up, because no sooner than the ringing stopped, it was starting right back. Visibly irritated he pulled it back out and answered, finally raising his gun with a warning look.

"I'm in the middle of something ma-. Wait. What?!" He barked. I watched as pure rage washed over his face from whatever Ms. Rachel was telling him. His voice even changed as he shot out different questions each more frantic than the last. "When did this happen......Was he alone....shit! What hospital...? Ayite I'm on my way now." He hung up and darted across the room so quickly that I wasn't prepared when he snatched me up by the arm. "I swear if I find out you and that nigga had anything to do with this...."

"I-I didn't." I stuttered shrinking away as he stood over me with flaring nostrils and red eyes. He stared me down briefly, I guess trying to decipher whether I was being truthful or not.

"We need to get to the hospital." He finally mumbled tucking his gun and dragging me out of the house behind him. A mixture of fear and love had me climbing into his truck instead of running away like I probably should have. Whatever was going on, he obviously needed me and since I'd fucked up so bad I was going to be there.

After mustering up the courage to speak, I waited until he began driving to ask. "Who's at the hospital?" He'd been silently texting away on his phone as he whipped through the streets, but my question had him squinting my way.

"Juice....Juice and Yo'Sahn-."

"What! You didn't think I needed to know that?" I shrieked cutting him off as tears sprang from my eyes. I felt like shit knowing that my sister had probably been trying to tell me, but I'd ignored her and left my phone in the car.

"I just told you, didn't I?"

"Okay, so what happened? Are they okay?" I didn't know how severe things were, but I was already praying that they were going to walk away unscathed.

He released a deep sigh and focused on the road before saying. "I don't know. They got shot outside of Yo'Sahn's school."

"Oh my God! I know Destiny's going crazy. Give me your phone!" Not waiting for him, I snatched it from where it was resting in his lap and dialed up my sister. I wasn't surprised when she didn't answer, but it didn't stop me from growing more concerned as I called her back only to get her voicemail once again. "Ughhhh! Why won't she answer!"

"Chill, we right here," Elijah grumbled taking the phone from my hand and just like he'd said we were pulling up to the hospital a second later. Before he could stop the car completely, I jumped out and ran into the emergency room entrance.

"I'm lookin for my nephew. His name is Yo'Sahn-." I started once I reached the nurses' station.

"Dream!"

Turning around, I saw my sister approaching with Ms. Rachel right behind her. As soon as she was within arms reach, I pulled her into a tight hug, both of us sobbing uncontrollably. "What happened? Are they saying anything?" I asked after embracing Mrs. Rachel too.

"I don't know! Juice was dropping Yo'Sahn off at practice, and there was a drive-by! The ambulance just brought them in not too long ago, but they haven't said anything yet!" Destiny cried wiping away tears only for another fresh set to cover her face.

"I'm so sorry this happened boo. They're going to be okay though I know it." I tried to speak words of encouragement even though my stomach was flipping with worry. Wrapping my arms around her shoulders, I said a silent prayer as Elijah walked up.

"Ma, how is he?" He hugged her and asked glancing my way briefly before focusing back on her. I shuddered knowing that we still hadn't figured out our situation and now we were dealing with this. While they talked, I prayed, and my sister cried. Elijah already was on a rampage, and if anything happened to his brother or Yo'Sahn, I knew it was only going to be worse.

DESTINY

I was exhausted from stress and crying, but I wasn't closing my eyes until I heard something about my baby and Juice. We'd been in the waiting room for hours, and I was stopping every nurse and doctor looking for an update. Dream and Mrs. Rachel, whose husband had finally arrived, had gone to get some food while Elijah stood off to the side talking on the phone. He'd been making all types of calls and ripping people's heads off this whole time, even their friend Trell who'd shown up not too long ago. I could tell that something was going on with him and Dream just from how distant he seemed from her, but they were keeping it to themselves because of the obvious.

Unable to sit any longer, I stood and began pacing. It felt like the walls were closing in on me. I just wouldn't be able to handle it if Yo'Sahn or Juice didn't pull through. All of our petty beef seemed so stupid at the moment, and I wouldn't be able to live with myself if his rude ass died.

"Family of Ye'Shan Parker and Jeremiah King?" A doctor finally emerged from the double doors butchering my baby's name.

He'd barely entered the waiting room, and I was on him like white on rice. "*Yo' Sahn,* Yo'Sahn Parker and we're right here. I'm his mother." I let him know as we all crowded his space.

"Oh- uh sorry about that." He said, clearing his throat uncomfortably. "I'm Dr. Gray, and Yo'Sahn and Jeremiah were both brought in with multiple gunshot wounds. It seems that Jeremiah took the brunt of it and was hit a total of three times. Once in the shoulder, once in the stomach and a superficial shot in the leg. We were able to remove each of the bullets without any problems, and he's resting comfortably. Now Yo'Sahn was only shot once in the arm. He did suffer a slight fracture in his radius as a result." Pausing he flipped the page up on the chart he held and pushed his glasses up his nose. "I set it with a cast, and it will be completely healed within six weeks. He also had a small head trauma from the fall, but I suspect he'll recover just fine. However, I would like for him to stay overnight for observation."

"Oh thank God! Can we see them?" I was crying tears of joy, and if Elijah hadn't been right there, my knees would've given out.

"Yes, Jeremiah is heavily sedated so he may be in and out, but Yo'Sahn is up, and he's been asking for you." He let us know shaking our hands before giving us their room numbers and disappearing back the way he came.

I went to grab my purse and stuff from my seat, ready to see both my babies when Antonio stepped into my line of sight. Anger washed over me as I took him in, even more upset at the fact that he had his latest fling on his arm.

"Oh hell no! What the fuck are you doing here!" I snapped charging in his direction.

"Why wouldn't I be here, that's my son back there, right? The school called me just like they called yo stupid ass!"

"Don't get fucked up in here Antonio, you know I don't play like that! Talkin bout the school called you fuck outta here, yo ass ain't been worried about Yo'Sahn. I'm gone need you to keep that same damn energy! You need to leave and take this raggedy-ass hoe with you!" I looked her up and down, ignoring the way she rolled her eyes.

"Hold up who you callin' a raggedy hoe, bitch!" She sneered taking a step towards me, but she was saved by Antonio holding her back. Today was the right day to try me because I was all too ready to lay her ass out.

"I'm callin' you a hoe! I dare you to bring yo ass over here and do something about it!"

"Aye man chill the fuck out! We ain't here for all that!" He said, giving her a stern look.

"Well, what are you here for then?"

"Yeah what the fuck you doin' here?" Dream and Mrs. Rachel walked up, holding bags of Burger King with her husband right behind them. She was just as displeased with his presence as I was, and it was clear by the way her face balled up as she came to stand beside me.

"This ain't even got shit to do with yo ass!" He spat. "I came to see Yo'Sahn. You better hope I don't take him since you obviously can't keep him out of harm's way! You think I ain't heard about how Juice been toting him around like he's his daddy! He probably got caught up in his bullshit, and that's why he's here now!"

"Bitch, Juice been more of a father than you've ever been! And I wish you would even think about trying to take MY son, nigga I'll kill you!" By now we'd drawn the attention of everyone in the waiting area, but I didn't even care. When I said I'd kill that nigga I meant just that! I would go to war behind Yo'Sahn! Before I could attack him like I wanted to Elijah came over, standing in front of me and blocking my path.

"Aye, bruh get the fuck on! Don't ever speak on my brother name. King problems ain't the kind you want!" He growled instantly making Antonio pipe down. Narrowing his eyes, he looked between Elijah and me backing away slowly.

"You already know this ain't over." Antonio's voice came out shaky once he was at safe distance away. "I'm coming for my son Destiny."

"Man if you don't…" Elijah started towards his retreating frame as Mrs. Rachel jumped in his way and pleaded.

"Elijah please!"

She held him back while Antonio's scary ass scrambled away and I was almost a little sad that he didn't get his hands on him. I couldn't even remember the last time that I'd saw his ass, and he had the nerve to come up there like he had rights to our son. The whole thing had me so mad that I was shaking.

"Son, let's go check on your brother and Yo'Sahn." Mr. King came up beside Elijah placing a hand on his shoulder. The mention of seeing Juice brought him out of his trance, and he gave a short nod finally turning away and filling his parents in on the doctor's update. Of course they were overjoyed, and we all made our way to the rooms.

Destiny and I headed to see Yo'Sahn first while everyone else went to see Juice. As soon as I laid eyes on him, a fresh set of tears flooded my face. He was sitting up in the hospital bed with a cast on his left arm and an irritated look on his face that dropped as soon as he saw me.

"Yo' Sahn!" I ran over and hugged him tightly, careful not to hurt his arm.

"Hey, baby." Dream choked out, leaning in for a quick embrace.

"What's up Ma, hey teetee. Is Juice okay?" He looked up at me hopefully as I sat down next to him and moved his dreads out of his eyes. "I tried to ask the doctor, but he wouldn't tell me nothing."

"Yeah, he's fine. I was gonna go see him after I checked on you." I kept planting kisses on his face happy that after hours of confusion, I was able to touch and talk to him. Antonio had come and fucked up my good mood but seeing my baby up and talking instantly put me at peace.

"Can I come too, before we go home?"

"I have to check with the doctor first, but you're staying the night so they can make sure you don't have a concussion," I told him thumbing away the smudge of red lipstick I'd left on his cheek. It was like I couldn't stop fawning over him, but I couldn't help it.

"I gotta see him! If he ain't jump on top of me, I would've got way more than a broken arm! Please let me go too. I gotta thank him!" The look on his face melted my heart. Up until that moment, I hadn't known any specific details about the shooting, but knowing that Juice had literally taken bullets for Yo'Sahn had tears misting my eyes. Dream and I shared a look, and it was obvious that she was thinking the same thing as me.

Yo'Sahn was still pleading his case even though my mind was made up. "Okay, okay we can go now, but you need to get a wheelchair cause I'm not bouta have you falling out on me," I warned pressing the button for a nurse.

"Mannn why you always gotta treat me like a baby." He fussed irritably, not realizing that he looked just like a baby the way he was pouting.

"Well, stop acting like one, and we won't treat you like it." Dream chimed in poking his good arm making him chuckle. A second later, the nurse came in with a cup of ice water for him and some Tylenol.

"Hello, I'm Tracey, and I'll be your nurse for the night. I went ahead and brought you something for pain." She smiled, and I could tell that I would like her off top.

"Thank you, can we get a wheelchair. He'd like to visit another patient before bed."

"Oh sure, I'll be right back." It didn't take her long to return with a chair for him, and before I knew it, we were being led down to Juice's room. The closer we got, the slower Dream seemed to walk, and I was reminded of the tension I'd seen earlier between her and Eazy. I made a mental note to ask her about it once we were alone. I just hoped that it wasn't because she'd took her crazy ass to see Budda.

"Annnd here we are!" Tracey stopped in front of Juice's door and tapped on it lightly before announcing herself and stepping inside. It was obvious that they'd been in a heated discussion before we got there just from the look on Eazy's face and how silent it became once we entered. Juice was sitting up and looking just as mean as ever but at the sight of Yo' Sahn he forced a smile.

"What's up lil man!" He beckoned us closer, and I stopped briefly as Ms. Rachel and Mr. King gave him kisses and a pat on the back. It was sweet how they had become so attached to him. It was like we had a real family besides just us three like it'd always been.

I took a moment to check Juice out and was surprised to find his eyes already on me. Every part of my body was longing to jump in his lap right then, but I held it together or at least I thought I did. His eyes gleamed and caressed me from head to toe like he knew exactly what I was thinking. That wasn't anything new though. Juice always gave me that look, that look that said he could eat me alive and it always sent an electric shock through me.

"Bring yo ass here Destiny." He stunned me, and probably everyone else in the room by saying. I took a few timid steps in his direction, and once I was close enough, he reached out grabbing ahold of my hand and pulled me the rest of the way until I was right next to him. He was looking at me so intensely that I couldn't meet his eyes.

"I know yo mean ass got something smart to say, but I just wanna thank you for protecting Yo'Sahn. I- I really appreciate you doing that." My voice cracked, and I closed my eyes to stop the tears that were threatening to fall. Juice didn't know how he'd saved more than just Yo'Sahn today; he'd saved me too. No one besides Dream and myself had ever looked out for him the way that Juice and Eazy had and I would forever be grateful for the way he'd stepped up with my son.

"Chill with all that, you know I'll do whatever for that lil nigga. If anything this whole shit happened cause the wrong muhfucka saw him with me." His features filled with guilt, and I automatically felt the need to comfort him.

"No, it didn't-."

"Nah, for real. I been having him with me like I ain't a walking target and I should've been more careful. I fucked up, and I'm sorry bout this shit man." He peered down to where Yo'Sahn had wheeled beside me with tears brimming his eyes. I'd never seen Juice show any other emotions besides anger and cockiness, and to see him so distraught was different to say the least.

"Don't say that big homie. This shit could've happened anytime, and even I know that." Yo'Sahn tried to reason, and I slapped his ass upside the head, forgetting all about the possible concussion. "Ouch, ma!"

"Watch yo mouth!" I gave him a stern look but rubbed his head gently.

He screwed his face up and put his attention back on Juice. "For real man, this ain't no big deal. I'm good, and I can get some of the shorties at the school to sign my cast." Juice finally cracked a smile at Yo'Sahn grinning like a fool. He didn't agree or disagree, so I knew he still felt bad as hell, but he wasn't trying to let it show. The conversation turned lighter, and I was glad to get a moment to gather myself. Today had been fucked up, but I was glad that they were both okay.

EAZY

"I don't give a fuck! Find that nigga today!" I fumed to one of our workers Deon and hung up before he could reply. I'd had niggas out scouring the street for Grim. He was basically Juice's shadow, and I thought it was funny as hell that he wasn't nowhere around during or after the shooting. A nigga felt helpless as fuck knowing my brother was laid up in the damn hospital, and I couldn't even find the niggas responsible. He blamed himself more than anybody else for what happened like we just had enemies all over the place, but I knew better. Things had been running smoothly, and while there had been slight issues here and there, neither of us had ever been shot before, so I knew there was more to it. And that most definitely started with Budda. As far as we knew he still had a week left before he would be released but I couldn't shake how suspicious it was that right when we'd found out about his past dealings with the police this shit happened.

"Bruh, I just spoke to my guy down at the jail and Budda's still there." Trell came into my office, shutting the door behind himself and taking a seat. "This gotta be somebody else."

"It's *not*," I grumbled angrily. "I know it's him, and you act

15

like just because the nigga behind the wall he can't have nobody touched. Just like our names hold weight his does too! Nobody knows about him ratting out his team, so niggas is still willing to do his bidding." I probably sounded straight out of a crime show to Trell, shit I felt like I was living a real-life conspiracy theory.

"Look you paranoid as hell right now, and it's fucking with the way you think. You gone fuck around and be looking in the wrong place and get caught slipping."

"I'm not paranoid muhfucka! You are underestimating that nigga and that's exactly what he wants! For us to not see this shit coming especially from him." Trell's eyes followed me as I paced behind my desk. I knew he thought I was crazy as hell, but shit was lining up for me, and all roads led back to Budda. With a growl, I knocked all of the papers onto the floor. I couldn't get my hands on who I wanted, so I was taking out my anger and frustration on any and everything else. For the past two days, I'd been murking niggas left and right. Some didn't even deserve it, but neither did my brother and if I didn't find out who was behind this shit, it was going to get way worse. Not only could my brother have lost his life, but Yo'Sahn could've died too, and that shit was eating at me. Add to that the fact that I wasn't speaking to Dream's sneaky ass and I was a raging bull.

"You need to go home and get some sleep or something. Yo ass look like shit nigga." Trell suggested, and I hit him with a nasty glare. I didn't need him to tell me that shit. I hadn't had a good night's sleep since the night before Juice got shot, but I just couldn't rest. Not when our whole operation and lives were on the line. For as prepared as I always thought I was this shit came out of nowhere and I had to admit that I was completely blindsided. That being said, I needed to get on top of it before anything else happened.

"I don't need sleep muhfucka; I need a nigga's head on a platter!"

"No, you need some pussy! Yo ass runnin' around more pressed about this shit than Juice! And he the one that got shot! Just like he said, this was probably random. How many niggas you know get shot out here on a daily?" He questioned, pausing for a second and continuing before I could speak. "Exactly! Plus, he said some lil niggas was out there right before the shit happened so honestly, it could've been them tryna clout chase."

I remained silent, brooding over how he and Juice were missing my stance on this. We'd already had this same argument at the hospital and hadn't gotten anywhere. Just like always, Juice swore he knew everything, even sitting up in a hospital bed with bullet holes in him. As far as me getting some pussy I could do without it, especially if it was attached to Dream! She had consorted with the enemy and even though I could tell that she didn't personally have shit to do with the shooting, her talking to Budda was enough of a reason to cut her off. If not the fact that she lied to me to do so! She was worse than Sherice in my eyes at this point, and she was lucky she wasn't dead.

I frowned inwardly. I wasn't even supposed to be thinking about her, but throughout the day, she always seemed to weasel her way into my thoughts. A knock at the door gave me the perfect opportunity to stop listening to Trell's dumb ass and hopefully get Dream off my mind.

"Come in!" I barked loudly, and the door opened, revealing one of the construction guys. He looked like he was almost afraid to step inside, but he did so anyway, taking in the mess on the floor and me looking like a ball of rage.

"Uh, Mr. King....? There's a young lady here to see you, and she's refusing to leave until she does." He stammered nervously looking between Trell and me. I can't lie, my chest tightened at the chance that it might have been Dream's lying ass out there and before I could stop myself, I was motioning for him to let her back.

"Nigga what?" I snapped because Trell was sitting there with his brow raised. He shrugged and slumped down into the chair as a timid knock sounded at the door. I was both surprised and irritated to see Sherice step inside, wearing a trench coat and a pair of red bottoms, that made her long legs look like they went on for days. At the sight of Trell, the smile slipped from her face, and she rolled her eyes.

"This bitch."

"*Bitch?* I got yo bitch nigga!" Sherice switched further into the room, and in his direction, angrily.

"Yeah, see a bitch point her out fuck! Keep talking crazy I'm gone give yo hoe ass what you looking for! I ain't this nigga right here!" They stood toe to toe, ready to rip each other's heads off, and I damn near wanted to let them.

"Tuhh, Can we talk in *private* Elijah?" she sneered never taking her eyes off of Trell. I stroked my beard, considering whether or not I should allow her a minute of my time.

"Gone head bro, I'll catch up with you in a minute." He cut his eyes my way, clearly wondering what the fuck I was on, but I didn't need him there monitoring my moves.

"Ayite man, don't do nothing stupid," Trell warned glaring at Sherice, before turning to me. "And when I say stupid, I mean anything that's gone piss Dream off." Grinning at the way her face tightened at the mention of Dream, he left clearly pleased with himself. I couldn't do shit but shake my head at his ignorant ass. The nigga knew damn well I wasn't fucking with Dream like that, but I didn't even bother to correct him or ease Sherice's mind about it either.

Once the door shut behind him, she quickly got herself together.

"Okay, so what do you want Sherice?" I questioned making

myself comfortable back behind my desk as she eyed my every move.

"I didn't realize that you and Dream were so…..serious." she tilted her head and I could see her attitude getting ready to make an appearance.

"Is that what you here for, to ask me shit about Dream, cause we can cut this lil chat short if you did," I replied dryly, busying myself with what was left on top of my desk. Honestly, the only reason that I'd let her ass stay was to take my mind off of Dream. The last thing I was trying to do was talk about her ass.

"Noooo, I actually came because I heard about Juice and I wanted to check on you." Sherice was laying it on thick and batting those long ass mink eyelashes as she came around and sat on the edge of the desk. She spread her legs and revealed her clean-shaven pussy underneath her coat, smirking once she saw me do a double-take.

"Really?" doubt was evident in my voice, knowing that she hated Juice and could care less about him being shot, but even with that knowledge I couldn't tear my eyes away from between her legs. It had been less than a week since the last time I'd been with Dream, but with the stress of our situation, plus the shit with Budda, I needed something to take the edge off.

"Yessssss," she purred. "I figured I should be there for you in your time of need. You look a little tense, and you know I'm a good stress reliever." In one swift motion, she untied the sash and let her trench fall to the floor, before getting down on her knees in front of me. She took my silence as permission for her to go ahead and unbutton my jeans. Since they were already slightly off of my waist, she was able to easily access my dick. With gleaming eyes, she pulled it free, wrapping her soft hands around it and inching it into her mouth. She was trying to take her time and be sexy, but I only wanted to feel her tonsils, so I grabbed her by the long curly ass weave she was wearing and forced her head down further. It only took her a second to adjust, and my dick stretched as it got harder, growing as she gagged and saliva ran down my balls.

"God damn, just like that," I grunted finally releasing my grip on her. With her eyes on me, she slurped and moaned squeezing my shit just right. If it was one thing this bitch knew how to do it was suck and fuck. She already had me on the verge of dumping my kids down her throat, and it hadn't even been ten minutes. "Get yo ass over that desk."

Happily, she pulled me from her mouth with a loud smack, wiping her face before bending over the length of my desk with one leg hiked up. I went right in one of the drawers and retrieved a condom, letting my jeans fall and quickly sheathing my dick. I might have been willing to fuck her, but I wasn't dumb enough to do the shit raw.

"Really, Elijah?" she lifted her head and sucked her teeth in disbelief.

"You want this dick or not?" I answered her question with one of my own, knowing she wasn't going to pass up an opportunity at fucking me again.

"You know I do."

"Okay then, shut the fuck up and take it how I give it to you!" Holding her leg in place, I ran my dick up and down her wet slit before easing my way inside of her. She was just as tight as I remembered, and it felt like she was choking my dick. The sound of her juicy ass pussy filled the room, mixed in with her cries and my occasional grunts. I was almost sure that she could be heard over the sound of the construction that was going on in the building.

"Ahhhh, fuck this pussy Eazy!" she hollered loudly as I rammed into her harder, gripping her waist tightly with one hand and thumbing her ass with the other. I bit into my bottom lip and tried not to bust as she squirted, soaking my dick.

"Shut the fuck up!" I ordered through clenched teeth, dipping lower so that she could feel me in her damn chest.

"I caaaaan't!" she whined. "You're too deep!" she was tossing her head from side to side dramatically and trying to claw her way over the edge in an attempt to run, but she wanted this dick, so she was going to take it. I was trying to fuck every one of my frustrations out on her, and I knew a big nut was on the horizon.

My eyes rolled into the back of my head as Sherice began to match my strokes, rotating her hips hypnotically and squeezing her pussy muscles at the same time.

"Ooooh shit! I'm- I'm cummmming!" her body trembled beneath me as an orgasm ripped through her, making her shriek loudly. I held her in place, feeling my own nut about to erupt, just as my eyes landed on the door. Seeing Dream standing there didn't stop me from delivering back-breaking strokes. If anything, her tear-streaked face only added to my pleasure, and I let loose into the condom with a loud ass growl. I grinned at her evilly as she backed away, hoping that she was just as hurt as I had been after finding out about her seeing Budda. I even added a little bit of flare by leaning down and planting a wet kiss on Sherice's neck.

When I finally looked up to see that she was gone a part of me was slightly disappointed that she hadn't come in here acting a fool, but I played it off well. Done with the show I tapped Sherice so she could get her ass up and out of my office.

She sat up out of breath and sweating despite the central air that was circulating the room. "Damn I missed that."

I turned my back on her, not trying to acknowledge the dumb ass smirk on her face. If she thought that this fuck made us a couple again she was highly mistaken, and I was ready to let her know just that until I noticed that the head of my dick was sticking out of the condom, dripping nut onto the floor. Angrily I ripped it off and trashed it, before pulling up my pants and snatching her off my desk by the arm.

"Hey- What are you doing?" she huffed fumbling to catch

her trench after I threw it her way. I almost didn't want to tell her stupid ass that I'd messed up and the fucking condom broke. Without a doubt she was going to be happy as hell, but little did she know we were headed to the nearest Walgreen's to pick up some plan B. I didn't care if I had to shove them down her throat, she was definitely about to swallow at least three of them bitches.

"Put that shit on. We gotta go get you a plan B."

Her face relaxed as she slipped into her coat and tied it back up with a shrug. "Oh, that's it? Come on then." She seemed rather happy to be killing her only chance to be connected to me, for life. I should've been concerned, but any rational thought was overshadowed by the fact that I wasn't trying to procreate with this bitch. So, instead of thinking it over too much I ushered her out the door, headed to fix this shit.

JUICE

*J*was supposed to be concentrating on beating Yo'Sahn's ass in Call of Duty, but Destiny kept huffing and puffing over in the corner as she texted away on her phone. Her face was scrunched up as she wrote what I was sure was a long ass paragraph, before mashing the send icon. Even as she sat there clearly upset, I couldn't deny how damn beautiful she was. It was like she was the most gorgeous when she had an attitude too. I'd been trying to figure out a way to let her know I wanted to fuck with her on some serious shit, but it just never seemed like the right time. Yo'Sahn had already told me about her talking to some new nigga, and I wasn't even tripping on that. She'd been up here with me every day when she wasn't at work so at least I knew she wasn't spending time with dude's ass. Still, I felt like I needed to hurry up and shoot my shot before it was too late.

"Yeah! Told you I was gone kick yo ass!" Yo'Sahn shouted bringing both me and Destiny's attention his way. His little ass had made five hundred kills to my twenty in the time that I'd spent staring at his damn mama.

"Boy I know you better watch yo mouth, 'fore knock all them teeth down yo throat!" she cut her eyes at him.

He grinned sneakily. "My bad ma."

"If she don't I'm gone knock yo shit loose, lil cheating ass!" I added making him fall out laughing.

"You gotta get up out that bed first crip!" he chuckled. "Don't be a sore loser tho my nigga, it ain't a good look on you." For his little ass to have his arm in a cast, he was talking cash money shit.

"Yeah ayite, don't let this hospital shit fool you, I'll hop up out this muhfucka and-."

"Make sure you hold the back of yo gown closed first!" he cracked, and I couldn't do shit but laugh. Even Destiny had to giggle, and I looked at her ass sideways.

"Fuck you laughin at?"

"Yo ass!" she said bucking and rolling her damn eyes as usual.

I chuckled with a slight nod of my head. "Y'all think shit gravy cause I'm up in this hospital bed, but a nigga ain't gone be down for long. Soon as I get up outta here, I'm putting both yall asses in a headlock." I warned making her laugh and wave me off. She could think I was full of shit if she wanted to, but the day they discharged me I was gone be on her ass. The bullets I took to my abdomen and shoulder were the most painful, but I could damn sure still use my left arm.

"Boy ain't nobody thinkin' bout yo ass *Jeremiah*, and I'm gone hit you right in the stomach as soon as you try me or my baby." The smile on her face told me that she was still playing, which she better had been. I only had two more days left in this hospital, and I couldn't wait to get discharged. Not only did I need to catch up with Jayden's bad ass, but I had to help Eazy figure out this shit with Budda. The nigga was driving himself crazy, and I knew that he needed me out there with him.

"Baaby!"

I was instantly put in a bad mood the second I heard Makalah come through the door screeching in that annoying ass voice. She was the last person I was expecting to see, but she waltzes her ass into my room, switching in her tight Fashion Nova dress and cheap ass heels. Without even looking, I could feel the attitude radiating off of Destiny from the corner as Makalah stopped in front of me and bent over trying to give me a kiss. I stiff-armed her ass, palming her whole face and giving her a small shove back.

"Juice!" she whined while I wiped her makeup off my hand and onto the sheets with a frown.

"You know damn well you don't put them crusty ass lips on me, fuck wrong with you?" she was still trying to brush off her embarrassment when I realized that Destiny was silently gathering her stuff to leave. "Aye, where you going?" I questioned, damn near breaking my neck to look around Makalah's dumb ass.

"I'm gonna take Yo'Sahn home, and I still need to get ready for work tomorrow anyway." She said, not bothering to bring her eyes my way.

"Yeah, it is about time you left. I'm here now, and I got him."

Destiny slipped her purse on her arm and turned around to face Makalah. "Girrrl, I'm gone let you make it cause my son is here right now."

"Man you ain't gotta go nowhere. I'm tryna talk to you anyway." I grabbed ahold of her hand and pulled her closer, ignoring the distress on Makalah's face. Nobody had invited her ass here anyway.

"Nah it's okay, we'll come back tomorrow-."

A knock at the door cut off what she was saying and in stepped the same detectives that I had been avoiding since the night I got here. I released a frustrated sigh and cursed under my breath. It made my ass itch anytime I was in the same vicinity as a member of law enforcement, but they were relentless. This was the fifth time that they'd stopped through here and every time I made an excuse not to even have a conversation with their asses.

"Destiny, you're just the person I wanted to see." The first one who entered grinned in her direction and said. Of course, they were familiar with her considering that she was here every time they came and she'd been present when they questioned Yo'Sahn.

Destiny looked between the two detectives before taking in the uniformed officer that snuck in behind them. "Ummm okay, for what?" I peeped Yo'Sahn stand up from his seat on the couch with his face twisted in a mean mug as if he already knew shit was about to go left.

"You're under arrest for the attack of a miss Gladys Taylor." He motioned for the officer to come forward as he tried to read her rights to her.

"What! I didn't even touch that old crazy bitch!" Destiny shrieked angrily snatching away the second the nigga put his hands on her.

"Well, we have more than five witnesses plus the video that says you did, now please place your arms behind your back and stop resisting." The detective still held a grin on his face like he was enjoying this shit way more than he should have been.

"Aye man yall niggas trippin'! Her shorty right here and shit, y'all ain't even have to do this here!" I fumed watching helplessly as they cuffed her and Yo'Sahn struggled to get to his mother while the other detective held him back.

"Oh, so you're up for speaking today, Mr. King? Because Miss Taylor made some serious allegations against you and Destiny here in regards to her grandson."

"Nigg-!" I grunted trying to climb out of that bed and knock his shit loose, but the sudden movement sent a sharp pain through my stomach that sat me right back down.

"Juice! What are you doing? Stay in bed." Makalah's high-pitched tone grated on my nerves as she called herself trying to calm me down by rubbing my arm.

"I'll be fine, y'all calm down," Destiny spoke making eye contact with both Yo'Sahn and me before she was carted out the door. I was highly pissed and ready to tear some shit up, but I kept my cool as best I could under the circumstances.

"So, now that that's out of the way. Can you answer some questions-?"

"Man fuck you! I ain't answering shit if you wanna talk to somebody call my fucking lawyer!" I spat. This nigga thought he was real funny coming in there and pulling that bullshit. If I wasn't planning on talking to him before, then I definitely wasn't about to talk to his ass after he arrested my bitch. He smirked and gave a curt nod before disappearing the same way he came.

"Juuuuice!" Makalah seemed surprised when I snatched away from her dumb ass.

"Don't fuckin Juice me! Make yourself useful and give me my damn phone!" I snapped at her before turning to Yo'Sahn who was still standing there with frustrated tears running down his face. "Its cool lil homie, we bouta clear this shit right up," I assured him as I dialed up our attorney. If I had to discharge myself out of this hospital, I was going to make sure that Destiny brought her ass home today.

AN HOUR LATER I WAS PULLING UP OUTSIDE OF THE POLICE station with Eazy and our lawyer Smith in tow. He'd brought his ass up to the hospital once they called and told him I was trying to discharge myself. I guess he called himself trying to talk me out of it, but as you can see, that didn't work.

"Mannnn, fuck is this bitch doin up here?" he grumbled once we got inside and saw Dream sitting in the waiting area.

"Be cool with that shit Eazy. We ain't here for that." I'd been

27

told all about the shit that happened between them, and in my opinion the nigga was overreacting, but he wouldn't listen to shit I had to say on the matter. Honestly, if he wanted to let his shorty go because of some stupid shit like that without letting her explain, then that was on him. My near-death experience had me seeing shit differently, and I wasn't trying to waste any more of the time I had on this earth.

"Jeremiah! Thank God you're here, they won't tell me shit besides that she doesn't have a bond!" Dream jumped up, ignoring the shit out of Eazy as she came over to us.

I knew that shit bothered him even though he tried to play it smooth, he was staring her ass down. "Yeah I'm bouta handle it. Smith." I nodded for him to get to work, and he made his way over to the desk to converse with one of the officers behind it.

Not even two minutes later, we were being escorted into an interrogation room where they were holding Destiny.

"Detectives, I believe this interview is over," Smith said with authority. Only one of the detectives from the hospital was inside the room, and the other was a woman I'd never seen. It was obvious that they had tried to bring her in so that she could try and get my girl to talk by relating to her. While the fake ass Stabler stood up damn near foaming at the mouth, Benson kept her eyes on Destiny.

"Come on, D." I held my hand out to her ready to get the fuck up out of there. Surprisingly, she was much calmer than I thought she'd be. Instead of tears and nerves, she came over to me like she hadn't just been being interrogated about a murder. Although she didn't really know anything besides that I was involved somehow, she still kept her cool better than some niggas I know.

"Now wait a damn minute!" Stabler tried to buck but was quickly shut down by Smith.

"You're going to need to lower your voice! Not only was my client illegally held even though she had a bond, but you're questioning her in regards to something that has nothing to do with the reason she is here. Now if you don't want a harassment suit, I suggest you back off detective Jones."

Stupefied the detective I now knew as Jones opened and closed his mouth lamely. I hit his ass with a smirk and ushered Destiny out the door with Smith right behind us. I wouldn't be surprised if he was able to get us out of there without me even having to pay the bond, he was just that good.

"What the fuck are you doing out the hospital, and where's my baby?" Destiny looked up at me from her spot under my arm as we made our way back to the front desk.

"Damn, you can't just say thanks for coming to get me Juice, you gotta jump right down my throat and shit? I thought I had saved the day and was gone get some fire ass head or something." I simpered only half-joking. For the second time today, she waved me off just as Dream screamed her name snatching her attention. They ran to each other like they were on the *Color Purple* or some shit while I spoke briefly with Smith.

It didn't take long for me to get her bonded out, especially since none of them wanted a lawsuit after the way they'd treated Destiny.

"Call me if you need anything else," Smith said shaking my hand. "And Destiny you shouldn't have any more problems out of them, but if you do…" He pulled a card out of his pocket and tried to hand it to her, but I quickly intercepted that shit. I could already see the gleam in his eyes as he took her fine ass in. Smith was cool and all, but he was definitely barking up the wrong tree.

"Nigga I got yo number." I shoved his card back in his hand as he chuckled before nodding and walking off. Destiny let out one of those girly ass giggles, and I shot her a look. "Fuck you keekee-ing about?"

Groaning, she rolled her eyes. "Nothing Juice. You need to calm yo hostile ass down and go back to the hospital! You should've never left anyways. Eazy how you let him check himself out? I'm telling Miss Rachel on both of y'all!" She slapped Eazy on the arm, making sure not to hit me because of my injuries.

"Aye, you the one got arrested for beatin' up old bitches and shit. I can't control this nigga, especially when you and Lil man are involved." Eazy huffed. "And you can tell my mama if you want to she know this nigga hard-headed."

I glared at the both of them with my face frowned up. "Stop talking bout me like I ain't right here, man."

"Destiny you ready to go?"

The attitude that was radiating off of Dream had me looking between her and Eazy curiously. He seemed just as irritated as she was, trying to pretend like he was busy doing something on his phone, but I knew he wasn't.

"Yeah, we done here right?" He finally cast his eyes upward making Dream suck her teeth.

"Y'all niggas trippin-."

"Nah it's cool Juice, I do need to get home and shower anyway. That fuckin police station dirty as hell." Destiny cringed like she'd really been anywhere besides in an interrogation room. I wanted to find out what all they'd had to even question her about, but I figured it could wait. If they didn't press formal charges, then it couldn't have been too much, so I'd catch her later when I dropped Yo'Sahn off.

"Ayite I'm gone bring lil man home in a minute." The look I gave didn't leave any room for argument even though I knew her ass wanted to argue.

"Ugh fine!" She walked off with Dream in tow mumbling that I was an asshole under her breath. I was gone let her slide this time, but I was definitely gone get her ass for that later.

DREAM

*E*ver since my dumb ass had gone to see Budda, I'd been paranoid as hell. I knew now that he had lied about the shit with Eazy, but the fact that he even knew enough to say something scared the fuck out of me. It meant that he had somebody watching me or at least feeding him some type of information and that wasn't good. I wanted to explain things to Elijah, but Jeremiah and Yo'Sahn getting shot quickly put a hold on that. He was so mad that he wasn't trying to talk to me anyway and I'm sure that the only reason he didn't suspect anything was because Yo'Sahn got hurt too. What he didn't know was that Budda didn't give a fuck about my nephew, so if he had been behind this, then he wouldn't have cared one way or another if Yo'Sahn had died. Like an idiot I'd swallowed my pride and tried to go and talk to Elijah once I felt like he'd calmed down, only to see him fucking his crazy ass ex. He might have been mad about me going to see Budda, but he definitely took that shit too far. And the fact that he saw me there and made no attempt to stop or anything! That was lower than low, and I was done with his ass. I'd rather let Budda kill me than to go to Elijah for protection, and that was on everything I loved.

"Who the hell is Shay?" Gabby entered the salon holding a huge bouquet of red roses with a confused look on her face. My heart pounded in my chest at the sound of my middle name. Only Budda called me that. While everyone looked around, trying to figure out who the flowers were for I tried to swallow the lump in my throat. Of course this nigga knew about the salon, he knew everything. I stopped combing through my client Shana's hair and hurried over to Gabby just as she started trying to read the card out loud.

"I'm Shay, thank you." I gave her a phony smile and snatched the fancy vase out of her hands.

"I thought yo name was Dream tho."

Fighting the urge to curse her nosy ass out, I simply gritted my teeth and said, "Shay is my middle name." I was already on my way back over to my station as I read the card to myself.

Dear Shay,
We left off on a bad note
So here are some roses
I know they're still your favorites.
Love always, Daddy

Even though I really wanted to tear the shit up, I kept my cool and sat it on top of my station with the flowers. Budda knew damn well roses were not my favorite flower, shit I didn't even like flowers. This shit was just to let me know that he could find me if he wanted to and it had done the trick because I couldn't even stop my hands from shaking as I got back to Shana's head.

"Oooh, Eazy so romantic!" Gabby gushed as she made her way over to her chair. The entire salon swooned too not even knowing that Eazy hadn't sent me shit and I didn't bother to correct them. Right now, only our family knew about our situation, and thankfully Destiny was in the back, and Mrs. Rachel wasn't here today. I'm sure they wouldn't have said nothing either, but it was nice not to have them looking at me in pity. Well until later anyway cause I knew Destiny's nosy ass was going to ask me about the flowers.

"Girl I'm gone need whatever prayer you used cause you definitely got that man wrapped around your finger." Shana teased, and I just shook my head. This bitch didn't even know what she was talking about. She just saw some damn roses and thought I had my nigga's head gone. These could have been some *I'm sorry for beating yo ass* roses for all she knew. I pretended to be one of those happy in love ass women and giggled, even though I was both shaken and pissed at the same time. Shaken because Budda was sending me messages and pissed because Elijah wasn't half of what these bitches were claiming him to be. It was so much shit going on in my life I couldn't even get my emotions in check.

Thankfully, a second later everybody was heavily engaged in a gossip session that I would have normally deaded, but I was so grateful for the attention to be off of me that I didn't even say shit.

I managed to get through the three clients I had scheduled, plus a few walk-ins by the end of the day. It was prom time, so we had a lot of teens coming in to get themselves together. Seeing them all brought back memories of when I was back in high school. It was an exciting time in a young person's life, and just their energy and happiness put me in a better mood.

"Bitch, who sent you these?" Dream asked the dreaded question as we prepared to leave for the night.

"Ugh, Budda. I been waiting for everybody to leave so I could throw them bitches away." I rolled my eyes with my lip turned up in disgust.

"Wait-what? You mean he sent those *here?*" She seemed just as alarmed as I did at first before her face twisted into a frown.

"I swear these niggas in jail got connections. He probably paid somebody all of his noodles for that favor."

"Girl, I'm not bouta play with you today."

"I'm just saying," she shrugged. "But for real though, you need to be careful. Eazy already pissed about you talkin' to that nigga. He finds out you getting roses and shit it's gone be even harder for y'all to get back right." She advised watching me closely as I dumped them into the trash. I still hadn't told her about me catching him with Sherice. It was obvious that she still held out hope for us, and honestly, I had hope too until I walked into his club that day. I didn't like involving my family in my relationship issues because I knew how awkward things could get after you inevitably get back together, but if I didn't tell her about what happened, she'd just keep bringing him up. Taking a deep breath, I explained about everything, including my volatile situation with Budda, ending on how I'd caught Elijah fucking Sherice across his desk like he had a reason to do so. Once I'd finished, she had a mix of different emotions cross her face as she started putting two and two together.

"Biiiitch I ought to slap the shit out of you! Why the hell would you go see a nigga that put you through so much! And I'm going to definitely get in Eazy's ass next time I see him! How the fuck he going try and do you like that! I mean I'd be mad too, but he took that shit too far and he ain't even heard your side of the story yet!" With her hands planted on her hips, she paced, as she ranted. Occasionally, shaking a finger in my face like she was the big sister.

"First of all, I told you I went to make him understand that I was happy and didn't want shit to do with him!"

"Yeah, and you see how that worked out for you! I *told* you not to go! When you're happy, you don't need to rub nobody's face in the shit. He didn't deserve an update on your life! And even if he did get out and come looking for you, Eazy would have handled that! Now you tryna tell me that this nigga is satan's nephew and you and your man done fell out! I'm bouta tell Juice!" My eyes bucked as she pulled out her phone ready to dial up Juice and bring a whole lot more drama my way.

"No! Don't tell him! You know he's just going to tell his brother, and I don't even want to see his ass right now!" I hissed snatching her phone from her hands and causing her to look at me crazy.

"So you'd rather deal with this nutty ass nigga Budda alone than to have Eazy help you?" She raised her brow incredulously, not bothering to take her phone back.

"I can handle Budda. It ain't like he getting out tomorrow or anytime soon for that matter." My voice held no hint of the actual fear I was feeling at the moment, and the more I talked, the more believable it sounded, even to me. Seeing that it wasn't convincing enough for her, I added. "Look, I got this ok, just... don't say nothing."

She studied me for what felt like a long time trying to see whether or not she should trust my word. Honestly I was more afraid to have to face Elijah than I was of Budda actually causing me harm at the moment and the irony of that wasn't lost on me. Just a week ago we were fine, making plans for vacation and all in love, yet he'd thrown that away because he *thought* he knew something that he didn't. All this time I thought I had the sweet brother, but I swear he was just as bad if not worse than Jeremiah's rude ass and if I never saw him again it'd still be too soon. It was bad enough he brought his ass up to the jail to pick up Destiny the other day, looking just as fine as always, like our break up hadn't hurt him too. I guess when you moved on as fast as he had then you didn't need time to mourn. Me, on the other hand, I was still reeling and trying to adjust and seeing him with that bitch Sherice hadn't helped at all.

Finally, Destiny released a heavy sigh. "Fine bitch, I'll keep them out of it *for now.*" She emphasized with a stern look snatching her phone back.

"That's all I ask."

"Yeah well let me find out it's more to it than you telling me and I'm gone testify like Tekashi." She grabbed up her bag in a huff while I picked up the bag with the roses and the mini backpack I'd worn today.

"I know you lying cause you ain't even say shit at the police station, but you'd snitch yo own sister out." Shaking my head in mock pity, I came up behind her as she reached the door.

"If it comes to yo safety then yeah I would… I'm not tryna see nothing happen to you and after Yoshi and Juice, I just can't take another situation like that." Already her eyes were watering at the thought, and I quickly pulled her into an embrace. I knew what the shooting had done to her so I wasn't trying to stress her out further when she'd just begun to act semi-normal.

"I promise I'm good boo. You just worry about my nephew and keeping Jaceon happy. I got my drama." I assured her.

Sniffling, she pulled away and rolled her eyes. "Girl don't even get me started on that nigga." After she got herself together, she helped me lock the door, and we walked together to the side of the building so that I could dump them damn flowers. It was a nice enough neighborhood, but we didn't want to take any chances.

Glad to finally get the focus off of me I asked. "What he do? I thought things were going good?" Just that quick her mood had shifted, and she let out a groan as we made it back to our cars.

"Nothin really, he's just been trippin about Juice and me spending time together. You know I was up at that hospital every day, and since he's been home, I make sure he's cool before I come here, but the only thing we got in common is Yo'Sahn at this point. I won't lie I thought about trying with him again but that bitch Makalah quickly reminded me of why we won't work. I'll forever be grateful for him but I ain't bouta play with his hoes." She was talking so fast that I could barely make out what she was saying, but that just meant that her ass was mad.

"Well, you and Juice got chemistry out of this world so he probably just feels threatened." I knew exactly what Jaceon was seeing when it came to my sister and Juice, especially since the shooting. She seemed to be the only one who couldn't see the shit, which was obvious by the blank ass expression on her face.

"Uh no, ain't no chemistry." Destiny fussed. "I barely like his ass as it is. Jaceon is doing too much, and I'm gone drop his ass if he don't let it go."

"Mmmhmm." I hummed, twisting my lips in doubt. I could already see where this shit was headed and she could too; she was just in denial.

"Don't mmhmm me. I'm for real."

"Oh, I'm sure you are, but I gotta go. I got an appointment at eight and I gotta run some errands before, so I'm gone need my sleep." Yawning I realized how tired I really was. I'd been throwing myself into work and trying to promote our business since Elijah and I fell out, and it was catching up to me.

"Fine I'll see you tomorrow but my first client ain't until noon." I'd noticed that she rarely scheduled clients in the mornings and I knew that had everything to do with Juice. Hiding the smirk on my face, I gave her an air kiss and a hug before we parted ways.

"Okay, love you."

"Love yo boring ass too." She tossed out over her shoulder before disappearing into her car.

I drove home on autopilot not really paying any attention to the direction, but about forty-five minutes later I was pulling up outside of my house. Today had been stressful as hell, and I couldn't wait to get inside and take off the uncomfortable ass heels I was wearing. The way my feet were aching made me miss the days of Elijah, giving me foot massages and warm baths, but I immediately shook those thoughts away. He wasn't thinking about me, so I needed to stop thinking about him. He was probably somewhere with his hoe ass ex while I was sitting in front of my house looking stupid. With that in mind, I locked up my car and trudged the short distance to my front door, stopping in my tracks at the sight of a sticky note attached to it. I looked around nervously, but nothing seemed out of place.

"Get it together, bitch. It's probably just a note from cable or something." I told myself, taking a deep breath and slowly reaching the door. Budda had me over paranoid, and my logical side had me chuckling at how extra I was being, but that turned into me choking once I read it.

You ain't have to throw those
expensive ass roses away
Stop testing me Shay!

DESTINY

"*G*o 'head answer that." Juice cheesed as he stuffed his face with the last of the loaded omelet, I'd cooked for him. I hurried and slid my phone off the table, making sure to silence the ringer as I stood up to clear our plates, but it was obvious from his smirk that he'd seen Jaceon's name. "You ain't gotta ignore the man on my account."

"Don't flatter yourself nigga, I just don't wanna talk to him right now." I lied glad that I had my back to him so he couldn't see it on my face. At first, I thought it was kind of cute how Jaceon would call to check on me throughout the day. I wasn't used to a nigga being so thoughtful and attentive. Back when I was with Dre, his ass barely gave a damn about my day or if I'd eaten for that matter. So to have a man be genuinely interested was … refreshing, but a call here and there quickly turned into five or more, and most of the time he was questioning me about Juice. When it first started I tried to reassure him that I was only helping the man out, I mean he'd saved my son's life! You'd think he'd be somewhat understanding about that, but all it did was lead to arguments because he took it as me defending Juice. He was being extremely immature about things and showing me a side of himself that I didn't really like, yet I was trying to give him the benefit of the doubt. Besides his jealous tendencies when it came to Juice, he was literally *perfect*. He was attractive, a business owner had a car and a house, and most importantly, he was cordial with Yo'Sahn. Those were all big pluses in my book, so I felt like I could overlook the minor shit, like him being jealous of Juice, but my patience with that was beginning to run thin.

"Oh, but you gonna answer his call when you leave though right?" His voice held a teasing tone to it, and I knew without looking that his ugly ass was smiling. "See he better than me, 'cause it ain't no way I'd let my woman be with another nigga and not answering the phone. Swear I'd pull up and air the whole shit out, matter fact she wouldn't even be at another nigga's crib cooking and shit anyway."

"Well, it ain't like that with us, so he don't have *nothing* to worry about." I said smartly knowing full well that I was lying through my teeth once again. It might not have been like that for him but contrary to what I'd told my sister I couldn't get Juice out of my system. I'd been doing a good job of hiding those feelings though, because despite what my heart wanted, my head knew better. I couldn't keep allowing his love for Yo'Sahn to mean love for me, that's why Makalah coming up to the hospital was such a good thing. Spending so much time with him, it was easy to fall under his spell, but the second his little fling showed up I was reminded of why we couldn't work in the first place.

"It ain't like what with us?" His question alarmed me for two reasons. One because he was asking about my feelings and two because he'd crossed the room and was in my personal space. I held my breath and tried to keep my composure, feeling him pressing against me as his lips brushed my earlobe.

"*Juuuuuice.*"

I'd meant for his name to come out sternly, but a bitch

moaned instead further amping up his already inflated ego. He wrapped his good arm around my middle and planted a light kiss on the back of my neck. It was everything I could do not to melt right then.

"God damn, I love the way you say that shit girl," he groaned clenching me tightly. "But that ain't answer my question." To be honest, I couldn't even remember what the hell he'd asked me at this point. Due to me trying to take things slow with Jaceon and not end up in the same predicament that I had with Juice it'd been weeks since I had any. Add to that the fact that I had somewhat strong feelings for this man and it was a recipe for disaster, but I couldn't stop myself from being sucked in. With the swiftness of a damn ninja, Juice had my pants unfastened and his fingers swimming in my wetness.

"Look at you, done already fucked up these panties cause you already know what it is. You might as well take em off."

I shuddered as he slid my pants down my legs and slowly ran his hand back up my thigh, before ripping my thongs off swiftly. He continued to talk his shit in my ear, while simultaneously assaulting my engorged and aching clit, turning me on to the point that my juices ran down my legs. "Mmmm." With a whimper, I threw my head back, resting it against his chest. Right when I felt myself on the brink of an orgasm, he moved away, leaving me panting and looking back at him with murder in my eyes. "What the fuck."

A wide grin spread across his face because he knew he had me right where he wanted me with his extra cocky ass. "Damn, I only got one hand shorty, I gotta get these shorts down." He joked, pushing his basketball shorts and briefs off his hips and releasing that mammoth-sized dick. It pointed straight at me looking good enough to eat. Since it had been dark the first time we were together, I didn't get a chance to actually see it and damn if I hadn't missed out. It was beautiful with its chocolate color and veins bulging the length of it. Pre-cum oozed out of its mushroomed head, and I couldn't miss the opportunity to taste it this time. I quickly stepped out of my pants that were pooled at my feet and dropped into a squat, lifting him into my mouth with both hands. That first drop was sweet and had me inching him further in, and moaning while I did. How I'd gone from making this nigga breakfast to sucking his dick in the kitchen I don't even know, but here I was. Slurping and slobbering trying to fit his entire length down my throat. His growls of pleasure further egged me on as he gripped my hair tightly.

"Fuuuuuck, suck that shit. Just. Like. That." With each word, he pumped hitting the back of my throat. I was even more turned on by his roughness, and I started rubbing my clit in a circular motion wanting to feel a release with him. "You bouta catch this nut like a big girl?" He looked down at me with glazed eyes and I moaned a yes while nodding. His dick pulsed and a second later he was filling my mouth with his seed. I didn't miss a beat though, I caught every drop and swallowed as I reached my own climax.

Juice didn't even give me a second to recover. Before I knew it I was bent over the very table we'd eaten at. He was already rock hard again, pushing my lower back down and poking at my center. It didn't take him long to fill me up, and we both released a satisfied sigh.

"This pussy still as good as I remember." He grunted as he delivered vicious strokes that felt like they were touching my soul.

"Juuuice, ohhh!" I reached back to try and stop him from going so deep, but he only gripped up my arm, holding it there.

"This my pussy Destiny, you don't tell me how to fuck it." *Lord, why did he have to say that?* The way his voice dropped and the authority in it had me creaming, and he still didn't let up. It felt like Juice was knocking my cervix out of place, but it hurt so damn good. Another orgasm was creeping up on me, and if it wasn't for the table, I would've collapsed. I trembled, holding on to the edge with my free hand as a wave of euphoria washed over me.

"Ohhh my gawwwd, I'm cummming!"

"Let me see it then, bust all on this dick!" As if he controlled my body, I came on his command, my juices gushing around him. "Fuuuck!" He released my arm, and instead grabbed ahold of my shoulder for better leverage as he drilled into me. I could feel his dick get harder and grow; a tell that he was about to reach his peak also. A couple of stiff pumps later and he was filling me with his cum. We both sat there panting for I don't know how long before the sound of my phone going off across the room broke me out of my sexually induced trance. Realization set in as Jaceon's ringtone filled the room and I hurried up and pushed Juice away. Of course, by the time I got to it, the call had gone to voicemail which was a blessing. In my panic, I was going to answer the phone with Juice's nut dripping out of me, on some straight dumb shit. This nigga had me going against things that I'd said I wasn't going to do and I needed to get the fuck away from him asap.

"Oh, fuck, fuck, fuck." I groaned, grabbing my pants from the floor. My ripped panties lay beside them unwearable, making me feel even worse.

"Destiny what the fuck is you doing man?" Juice faced me still completely naked since he'd never had a shirt on in the first place. Shamefully I avoided his eyes and rushed to the half bathroom next to his kitchen, slamming the door shut behind me and making sure to lock it. I cut the hot water on and looked at myself in the mirror, taking in my guilt covered face.

"What did I dooo?" I whined squeezing my eyes closed.

"You fucked yo future husband! What you trippin for?" Juice's voice sounded from the other side of the door as he simultaneously twisted the knob. "Fuck you lock the door for?"

I inwardly groaned and rolled my eyes. As bad as I wanted what he'd said to be true, I knew he was full of shit. Probably the only reason that he'd even been giving me as much attention as he had was because he saw me spending time with another man and niggas could never take what they dished out. Irritated I tried to relax as I found a towel and cleaned myself up, this was the second time that I'd allowed Juice to fuck me raw and nut in me. As I redressed, I made a mental note to make a doctor's appointment later. It was already going on eleven, and I had a client scheduled soon. There was no way that I would make it home to shower and change and get to the shop in time. I'd just text my client and tell her I was running late. Juice was still at the door when I finally emerged fully dressed and ready to forget this whole thing ever happened.

"Destiny what the fuck bruh!" He snatched me back to him roughly when I tried to get past.

"This shouldn't have happened! I got a whole ass nigga, that don't deserve this. Yo ass don't care though right as long as you got what you wanted!"

"You wanted that shit too, don't try and put this on just me! We *both* wanted it so again why Yo ass trippin'?" I fought back the tears as he eyed me, looking completely confused about how quickly my mood had shifted.

"You're right, that was my fuck up because I know you don't intend to do right by me and I just let you make me risk something good just for a nut. I gotta go, Jeremiah. Make sure you take your meds." With that, I pulled away, and this time he let me go, not bothering to stop me. I was glad Yo'Sahn had gone back to school because I didn't want to risk him asking me questions once he saw my tear-streaked face. Though, if he wasn't at school, this whole thing probably wouldn't have happened. Thankfully, that was something that I didn't have to worry about. The bigger issue was trying to act normal once I did speak to Jaceon.

EAZY

$\mathcal{I}$t had been days, and we still didn't have any word on the shooting or the whereabouts of Grim. The nigga didn't have any family besides his girl, and in an effort to draw him out I'd been made the call to kidnap the bitch. She was one of them nerdy type of females, went to school and worked a regular nine to five. I wasn't sure what she was doing with a nigga like Grim because it was clear that she wasn't built for the street life. It took her less than a minute to start spilling her guts, and she didn't even have anything valuable to tell, besides that the last time she'd seen him was the morning that Juice got shot. That lined up perfectly with him being involved somehow, whether it was directly or not. Niggas don't just go from being by your side almost every day to dipping when things get tough, and it definitely wasn't like Grim. Even though I believed her, I still sent a hollow tip through her skull. At this point she was a weak link, and I didn't fuck with those. I'd given up my reckless ways, a long time ago and I wasn't actually very wild, but my brother and Yo'Sahn being shot plus the shit with Dream and Budda awakened a whole different type of beast. Getting my hands dirty was rare for me. My name rang bells that made it possible for me to give orders and have people touched on my behalf, yet here I was busting my gun.

"Dammn, the bitch was in the middle of a sentence nigga!" Trell quipped inspecting the wound in her head, while Juice stood by silently. The look on his face let me know that he was trying to process what she'd told us.

"She wasn't talking about shit!" I huffed motioning for Cal and Ro the two niggas who worked for us, to get her body and dispose of it. My patience these days was limited. I wasn't beat to play games with anybody, and I wasn't leaving any loose ends.

"Swear to God since you fucked Sherice yo ass been crazier than usual! I think some of her mental disorder rubbed off on you my G." I hadn't talked about or really thought much of what had happened with Sherice and me simply because it was just sex for me. I'd needed a nut, and she was there, it was as cut and dried as that.

"Nigga you fucked that triflin' hoe after what she did?" Juice finally snapped out of his trance and looked my way in disbelief.

"Hell yeah, and Dream walked in on him too." Trell shook his head and laughed as we all watched Cal lift old girl up on his shoulders, while Ro got rid of her purse and other shit that she had on her when they'd snatched her up. I ignored the piercing glare that Juice was burning into the side of my head. My affairs were just that! Mine! I didn't involve myself in his shit, and I needed that same respect from him. Besides, I was the big brother, and he was the little brother, so his opinion was unwarranted.

"You out here wildin' bro! You that bothered by that nigga Budda?" he asked even though he knew I wasn't trying to have this conversation, but when had Juice ever been worried about overstepping his boundaries.

I absentmindedly looked down at my vibrating phone, ignoring yet another call from Sherice. She'd been blowing me up thinking that the episode in my office meant we were getting back together despite me telling her the opposite. "I ain't bothered by him at all. You and Trell making that shit bigger than it is. It was a fuck that's it."

A second after I sent her to voicemail again, she was sending me messages back to back. With a frown, I deleted them all without even reading what they said. Honestly, I should've blocked her, but I knew that she'd come in handy when I wanted to get some frustration out again. If she wanted to act like a hoe, I had no problems treating her as such.

"Do she know that? I bet she been blowing yo ass up since that shit happened." Trell said pausing so that I could try and deny the accusation. He busted out laughing when I didn't say anything, knowing that was exactly what she'd been doing. "See I knew it! You done fucked her and she thinks she's back in there. I told yo ass not to do it."

"Man fuck you!" pissed off about the accuracy in what he'd said I walked away so that I could pay Ro and Cal for their services. With Grim gone they'd been picking up all of the work, and I was throwing them a few extra bills, especially since I'd been killing people left and right. Once I had them squared away, we all left so that I could drop Juice and Trell's nosy asses back off to their cars and go on about my night. As soon as we got in the car though they both started back up with their shit. I immediately cut the radio up on them and ignored anything they said that had anything to do with Dream or Sherice.

Juice could talk all he wanted to, but he was still dealing with his own shit with Destiny. I could see the change in him as far as him actually wanting to be serious with one female, but she had already moved on. To be honest, I was surprised that he hadn't already tried to take the nigga out of the equation, but it was clear that he was doing things differently these days. His near-death experience seemed to have changed him. I was just hoping that it worked out for him in the end, unlike how it had for me.

The ride to their cars flew by, and before I knew it, I was dropping them off and on my way. I stopped off long enough to switch cars, opting for a beater and leaving my shit at one of the traps. Since neither Trell nor Juice wanted to believe that Budda could be behind this and we were quickly reaching his release date I decided that I'd drop in on the warden from Statesville. He'd been giving that nigga special treatment from day one, and I always figured it was because of Budda's clout. I was starting to see that everything around him was shady business though, and there was much more to it than just his name alone. After all of the snitching he'd done, he was damn near on the police force, and all of his freebies were coming from their allegiance.

It was late, so all of the lights were out when I pulled up to the huge mansion that rivaled my own. I couldn't lie, I was impressed knowing that his income couldn't afford him a place of this stature, but it was obvious he was into other shit. How his colleagues didn't know was beyond me, but that wasn't my problem.

With my car still running I sent a text to that nigga's maid letting her know I was outside. Warden Walsh had a thing for young black girls, so his entire staff consisted of the best that the hood had to offer, and regardless of how much he paid them, they wouldn't turn down no extra money. The cool $10,000 that I'd offered her was enough to get her to cut the cameras, disarm the alarm and seduce her boss long enough for me to get in. Not even a second later, she was messaging me that everything was set up as I slipped on a pair of gloves.

I cut the ignition and crept up just as the gate opened to allow me entrance. The all black that I wore made it easy to blend into the darkness, as I eased up the long driveway and to the front door. I stepped into the foyer and tried to let my eyes adjust before heading towards his office located in the back.

The light illuminated from under the door and spilled out into the hallway as I got closer. I could hear him moaning for the girl, Nique, to spank him and I instantly frowned when it sounded like she did as he'd asked. Disgusted I pushed the door completely open and stepped into the room to see Warden Walsh bent over a chair with his pants around his ankles. Nique was gearing up to deliver another smack to his ass when I made my presence known.

"Aye, stand up and pull up yo damn pants nigga ain't nobody tryna see this shit!" I based pissed off about having walked in on that shit. Nique backed away and faked a look of alarm, while the Warden quickly stood to his feet and struggled to get his pants up. His face was bright red as he looked my way angrily.

"What are you doing in here! How did you even get past the gate!" he fumbled with his belt, never taking his eyes off of me.

Shrugging I sat down on the couch beside his door and crossed my legs casually. "I have my ways. I'm actually here because I have some questions for you Warden. Now if you answer them truthfully, then I'll leave and go on about my night, but if you don't….well then you know." I lifted my gun from my lap with the threat.

"Listen, Eazy I-."

Pointing at Nique, I motioned for her to leave. "You can go," I said cutting him off midsentence. She discreetly nodded my way before hustling out of the room. The Warden looked after her probably wishing that he could leave too, but knowing he wouldn't make it far. A second later the front door slammed behind her, and we were left alone, he took that moment to begin to plead his case.

"If this is about Brian, I don't know anything." He backed away, loosening his tie.

"See, now I think you're lying. If you didn't know anything, then why would you bring his name up of all things?" my voice was calm despite the rage brewing inside of me. I knew that there was more to this shit, and he was going to be the key.

"I-I uh." He stuttered. While he tried to figure out what he wanted to say I pulled my silencer out and screwed it on casually, which made him even more nervous. I'd already told him the rules, and he was starting off on a bad foot by lying. Once I had it completely on, I shot him in the foot. Howling he fell back into the chair that he'd previously been bent over as sweat and tears poured down his face.

"I told you what would happen if you lied man. Is what you're hiding really worth dying over?"

"You don't understand!" he wailed jumping as I aimed the gun at various parts of his body.

"Well make me before I kill yo fat ass! I ain't got all day!" Like I'd said my patience had been running low as of late and I was ready to just go ahead and kill him because he was playing like I hadn't told him that I would. If I was nothing else I was a man of my word and this was the second time that he'd lied. Well, he hadn't really lied, but he didn't answer my question like I'd instructed him to.

"Oh-okaaaay!" I'd sent a bullet right past his head, just barely grazing his ear.

"The next one won't miss John."

"Brian is working with the Feds! They released him early because he promised to get them you and your brother in exchange for immunity. The problem is he's been MIA since then, and they still haven't made contact. My job was to make it appear that he was still inside until they found him."

I nodded already having been privy to what he was saying besides the fact of him having already been out of jail. Since he didn't know shit about my operation there was nothing he could tell the Feds about me. However, I did want to know one thing. Standing up, I made my way over and sat on the edge of his desk right in front of him. "So, I guess the million-dollar question is, when was he released?"

Fear covered his face, probably because he was aware that I wasn't going to like his answer. "About ....two weeks ago." He panted still holding onto his ear.

"See that wasn't so hard, was it?" Although the question was rhetorical, he still made an attempt to speak, and I quickly cut him off by shooting him twice in the head. There was no way I was letting him walk, and he was dumb to believe that I would especially after he gave me such a hard time at first. Shaking my head, I headed out sending a text to Juice and Trell. I'd been right this entire time and not only had Budda been out but he had one up on us for the last couple of weeks. I couldn't wait to catch his ass!

DRE

"We need to do this shit *now* nigga! You think they just gone let what happened to Juice slide! It won't be long before they find out I ain't dead and yo ass ain't in jail!" I was tired of waiting on Budda to come through with some type of action. Ever since he'd been home, we'd been holed up at one of his little slide's crib, and I was more than ready to leave. It had been his idea for me to lay low and not make my presence known thinking that it would give us a leg up, but since shooting Juice and Yo'Sahn we hadn't done shit! Well, aside from killing Grim and the little nigga Jayden. After a little consideration Budda felt like it would be best to get him out the way, he didn't want nobody being able to point the finger at me later on down the line, and I agreed.

"You talkin' like you really did something. You ain't kill him or the kid, so I don't know why you in such a rush to fuck up again stupid ass nigga!" He finally looked up from his phone long enough to say. His crazy ass had set up some type of tracking device on Dream's car, and he watched that shit almost faithfully. I couldn't figure out what he wanted with her stuck up ass, but that wasn't my issue anyway. If he wanted to stalk his ex, then that was on him as long as I didn't get caught up in the shit. I just wanted to get back on top and get to the money so Destiny could come crawling back once she saw me shining. I still wasn't sure if I would want her back after she'd been Juice's cum rag, but I had plenty of time to decide since we weren't doing shit.

"At least I did *something!* We need to strike while they're out here clueless! Besides, ain't yo homies lookin' for you too? What if they find you before we get at Eazy and Juice?" Mentioning the Feds had him quiet! Of course, they'd let him out early, and he'd gotten ghost the second they weren't around. I was cool with that plan when we were talking about our revenge, but now it just seemed stupid considering that he wouldn't have their protection either once Eazy found out.

"Stop sayin' them niggas my friends!" he spat finally finding his voice. Jumping to his feet, he stormed over to me and stood in my face angrily.

"Aye, chill out bruh-."

"You chill the fuck out! Yo ass talk too much muhfucka! Don't worry about what the fuck I got going on, you keep forgetting that I run this shit not you!" Spit was flying out of his mouth as he bent down, yelling damn near nose to nose with me. He had a crazed look in his eyes, and I didn't know how far he was willing to take this shit. I wasn't no punk ass nigga, but I didn't want the type of smoke that Budda could bring my way. Besides that, he was providing me with somewhere to live, so I needed to be cool unless I wanted to go and stay back with my granny.

"Ayite man calm down." I held my hands up in mock surrender, trying to deescalate the situation because Budda looked geared to go. "For real, my bad bruh." He was breathing heavily as he narrowed his eyes on me, before finally backing away as if my words had taken a minute to sink in.

"Look, I know you want to move, and we will, but when I

say so." He slapped a hand against his chest. "It's a reason why I'm the brains behind this shit, just....just give me a minute to iron out the details." Once again, I was ready to protest but the sound of the door slamming shut, silenced me. A second later heels clicked down the short hallway, and his girl Olivia came around the corner.

"What's going on here?" she asked, sensing the tension in the room, as she took us in. I can't lie Olivia was bad as hell. Her skin was a blemish-free caramel color, she had big brown eyes, with a slender little nose and plump lips. I often found myself staring at her fine ass, and she damn sure made it hard not to with her thick ass body. Even as she stood in the doorway looking at us curiously, my eyes roamed her body from head to toe. She had on some high-waist, black skinny jeans that emphasized her ass and tiny waist, with a white crop top, and a pair of strappy heels. Looking at her always made me wonder even more why Budda was chasing down Dream who didn't want him when he had her in his corner. I felt my dick twitch in my pants, and I knew I needed to get my ass on.

Budda backed out of my space with his eyes still on me. "Ain't shit, me and Dre just having a conversation." Although I didn't like the way he'd said that I didn't let it show on my face as I watched him walk over to her since it was obvious she didn't believe him. Doubt was clear in her eyes, but instead of saying anything, she allowed him to pull her into an embrace. I took that as my cue, snatching up the keys to the beater we'd been using and brushing past them to get to the door. I was glad Budda didn't bother to ask me where I was going because honestly, I didn't know, I just needed to get away for a minute.

It was still early, just past eight and I really didn't have shit to do since I was supposed to be laying low. I checked to see if Budda had left any weed in the glove box where he usually kept it and was pleased to see that he had. A second later, I was at the corner store grabbing a blunt to roll up with no fear of being spotted since Olivia stayed out in Blue Island, far as fuck away from my hood.

After perfectly twisting up my weed, I cut the music up and drove off with no real destination in mind. I was pulling up to Dream and Destiny's salon by the time I'd finished smoking, and I couldn't front anger bubbled up inside of me at the sight of what she'd done without me. I'd known that she wanted to open up a shop with her sister and that she had been saving for it when I took that money from her. Yet I never thought she'd have sent Juice after me for that shit. It wasn't like I wouldn't have gotten it back for her. I can't even front I was hurt and thought for sure that she had something to do with him coming after me the way he had, but more than anything it pissed me off.

I was damn near foaming at the mouth as I watched her and a few other females stand around talking inside the salon. She was looking all bright and bubbly, clearly not as depressed as I thought she'd be after my failed attempt at killing Juice and Yo'Sahn. It seemed like life had gone back to business as usual for them while Budda and I were around here, hiding and shit. I was so lost in my own thoughts that I'd barely realized when they all started leaving the salon and going to their cars. Instinctively, I reached for my gun once I saw Destiny come out and was pissed when I realized that I hadn't brought one with me. So, I had to watch her, and the others leave unable to fuck them up like I wanted.

I was still sitting there fuming when the thought to burn that shit down crossed my mind. Even if the shit didn't burn to the ground being able to fuck up what they'd worked for in some way would still feel like vengeance to me. I frantically looked around the car for something that would help me spark up a fire and didn't immediately see anything until an almost empty bottle of Grey Goose caught my eye on the floor of the backseat. I couldn't help but feel like it was meant to be for me to do this when I spotted that shit.

Right there in the front seat I tore my shirt into pieces and stuffed one part of it down through the mouth of the bottle, making a Molotov cocktail. Once it was complete, I made sure that no one was around, before popping the trunk and getting a tire iron out. Everything was still inside of the salon when I made it across the street, and I quickly smashed in the glass door, letting myself inside. What I wasn't expecting was for an alarm to start blaring, but I was too far to turn back now. I hurried to light the tip of my shirt and threw it into the middle of the floor. Flames began engulfing the entire floor and stretching to the chairs and stations. Satisfied with my work I watched for a second before making a mad dash back to my car, pulling off just as the sound of police sirens blared through the night. My heart was pounding so hard I thought my chest would cave, but even the fear of possibly getting caught didn't stop me from grinning maniacally as I drove back to Olivia's.

JUICE

I'd been looking all over for Jayden ever since I was well enough to get around on my own. With the way Destiny, Eazy and my mama hovered I couldn't get a moment to myself to check out my own leads. Eazy was dead set on Budda being behind the shooting, but he hadn't been there. I'd looked that little nigga in the eyes, and it wasn't shit there. He was a lost cause and didn't have shit but malice in his heart for Yo'Sahn. I saw the shit coming too, and despite me stopping them from hanging out together, he'd still managed to get at my lil homie. Since day one I'd had my suspicions about him and his friends, but Eazy wasn't trying to hear me.

Finding out that Budda had switched sides had Eazy's ass paranoid as hell and Grim going ghost didn't help. I myself felt it was a strong possibility that the nigga was dead. As hard as Eazy was going with the idea that he'd run off, it was just more likely with the life he lived that he'd gotten himself killed. Instead of listening to reason this nigga went and kidnapped the man's girl. I stopped even arguing with him about the shit because just like me he was gone do what he wanted to do. Even though he was wilding out, I had to admit that Grim disappearing the day of the shooting did have me wondering, but I still wanted to check out Jayden.

Since I didn't want Yo'Sahn knowing about my suspicions, I decided not to ask him any questions about his old friend. He was already in a weird place because he was going to miss the rest of basketball season and I didn't want to make it any worse by alluding to Jayden having anything to do with us being shot. I got Trell to look into it for me instead, and he'd just gotten the address for him today. We pulled up to the shabby looking, brick duplex with people littering the sidewalk and street out front. I immediately checked to make sure my safety was off because I wasn't taking any more chances and Trell followed suit.

"You sure this is it?" I asked eying the building and all the niggas around. It shouldn't have been a surprise for me considering the type of crowd I'd seen him with, but Destiny swore that his mama wasn't the type to be putting up with shit like this.

Trell shot me an irritated look and sucked his teeth. "Nigga yeah I'm sure. They live downstairs." He huffed, tucking his gun and reaching for the door.

"Shit I was just asking ole salty ass nigga." Grumbling, I climbed out of the car with him not too far behind me. As we reached the curb, all eyes were on us, and every conversation came to a halt. They cleared a path for us to get through, whispering amongst each other as we walked inside of the gate and up the concrete steps. I pounded on the front door since there wasn't a bell and a minute or so later a short, light-skin woman came out wrapped in a red satin robe and a bonnet. Through the glass, I could see her glossy eyes and the stagger in her walk, letting me know she was drunk, and I groaned lowly as she narrowed her eyes at me. Her attitude was already on twenty as she unlocked the deadbolt and pulled the door open with her face balled up.

"What the hell y'all niggas want!" she barked looking us up and down, smelling like she'd spilled a whole bottle of Hennessey on herself. I instantly turn to Trell because I wasn't about to deal with her smart-ass mouth.

He cleared his throat and put on his professional voice like his ass was calling to ask about a job application. "Umm, ma'am we were just wondering if Jayden is home-?"

"Fuck y'all lookin' for Jayden for? If he owes yall some money, I ain't got shit to do with that!"

"Lady ain't nobody said shit about him owing nothin'! We tryna talk to his lil bad ass!" I cut in once she started with her shit. I should've known it was gone be some bullshit just from the heavy smell of liquor on her, but I wasn't about to deal with her stank ass attitude. Her lip began quivering and tears welled up in her eyes, causing me to send a perplexed look Trell's way. He seemed just as confused as me and shrugged with a raised brow. We both watched confused as she wiped her face and sniffled gathering herself.

"Jayden is dead! So no, you can't talk to him! Fuckin' around with niggas like y'all is probably why I'm getting ready to bury him now! Get the hell from 'round here!" I was so stunned by her admission that I didn't have time to react when she slammed the door in our faces and went back inside of her apartment.

"Dead?" we said in unison, turning to each other. I started to knock again so that I could get some answers, but Trell stopped me and nodded at the crowd still standing around on the sidewalk. He jogged down the steps with me right behind him and stepped out of the gate approaching one of the dudes.

"Aye, yall know what happened to the kid that stayed here?" he pointed at the building we'd just come from, and I realized that one of these niggas had been with Jayden the night of the shooting. It seemed like the longer we stood there, his eyes began to light up with the same recognition widening in surprise.

"Wasn't you with Jayden that night at the school?" I squinted cocking my head to the side. The question had barely left my mouth when his ass tried to take off running. Despite the witnesses, I was willing to shoot him right in the leg since I couldn't run, but his clumsy ass did me a favor by tripping over his own damn feet.

"That's what yo lil stupid ass get nigga!" Trell laughed, pinning him down with a foot on his chest after he caught up to him. With my gun out, I limped their way as everybody else ran in different directions trying to avoid whatever was about to happen. By the time I got to them, Trell had hoisted him off the ground was holding him against the gate.

"Fuck you run for?" I was tired as hell from trying to rush over there and pissed off about such a distance tiring me out.

"Jayden said dude would pay us if we started some shit with y'all that day!" he spilled without me even having to ask.

Incensed I pressed my gun under his chin. "What dude nigga you need to be more specific!"

"I-I don't know! I ain't never seen him before! He pulled up on us right after with a big black nigga with dreads! Please don't shoot me bro!" Terror was written all over his face as he struggled to get his words out. I didn't plan on shooting him, but if the impending threat would make him talk then so be it. The mention of a big black dude with dreads, had Trell looking my way for a reaction that I wasn't going to give him. It was a million niggas fitting that description walking around Chicago every day. This kid saying the shit didn't mean it was Grim, but at the same time, it very well could've been him.

"So what happened to Jayden?" I asked as he sniveled damn near uncontrollably.

"Nobody knows what happened, he was supposed to meet us at the park, but h-he never came. His mama said he got shot right out front." Using his chin, he pointed back to Jayden's house. I hated to admit it, but that was a classic case of circumstances around here, it wasn't like niggas wasn't just going around shooting just because they could. Still, a big part of me knew that he got killed by whoever paid him to set us up.

"And you don't know who the nigga was he got the money from?" Trell's mind was headed in the same direction as mine and we both stared at him curiously while he raked his brain for something to give us.

"Ummm, uh…oh, oh! He said it was ole boy's mama ex!" he shrieked snapping his finger as it came to him.

"Huh?"

"The fuck?"

Trell and I said at the same time. I knew damn well he had to be confused or fucking high! Destiny's ex was dead! I'd been the one to kill him!

"He said-."

"Nigga we heard you!" I barked as a million different thoughts went running through my mind. When I'd left Dre with Grim, I knew his ass was dead, but now I wasn't so sure. And I also wasn't sure if I'd been wrong about Grim being dead. The last time I'd seen either one they were together and according to this kid's description they'd been the ones who shot me and Yo'Sahn too.

"Damnnnn, is this lil nigga sayin' what I think he sayin'?" Trell's eyes bucked out of his head as realization set in. I nodded, letting him know that it was exactly what he was thinking, and we both dropped a bunch of expletives. Nervously, the kid looked back and forth between us unsure of what was happening. "Get the fuck outta here!" Trell grit giving him a hard shove, he shot off down the street cutting through a yard and then disappearing around the side of a house.

I started back to the car angrily, knowing without even

looking that Trell was about to say something to have me ready to rock his shit. "Don't even start with yo shit bro."

"I wasn't even bouta say shit, but for real though.....how the fuck you ain't make sure that nigga Dre was dead? That's some rookie shit, wait til Eazy here about this shit!"

I stopped at the driver's door and gave him a blank face. He knew just like I did that Grim was supposed to finish that nigga off if he wasn't dead, before disposing of his body. I didn't know what reason he would've had to give Dre a pass out of all the niggas I'd had him get rid of for me, but it must have been good enough to make him switch sides. That shit was a problem in itself because it wasn't no telling how many times he'd done the shit, and Trell was over here making jokes. He had his phone out already typing furiously, no doubt running his mouth to my brother like a bitch as I got behind the wheel. My phone started going off just as I turned the key, ready to pull off and leave his ass right there. Seeing that it was Destiny I sent her to voicemail, I wasn't in the mood to deal with her emotional ass at the moment, but she called right back.

"Man, what you want-?"

"Juice! You gotta get to the shop right now! There was a fire, and we can't get ahold of Ms. Rachel!"

DREAM

*P*ulling up to see our salon engulfed in flames made my heart drop in despair. When I'd gotten the call from our security company I was scared, but I also was hoping for the best. The sight before me proved to be much worse than I could have imagined. Firefighters were everywhere working tenuously to put out the flames that had stretched to the building next door. It was utter chaos as other business owners and random people filled the street watching in horror while the police tried to keep them at bay. I spotted my sister, fighting to get past one of the barriers they'd set up, and I rushed to get over to her.

"Destiny!" I hollered once I was close enough. "Destiny!"

At the sound of her name, she spun around with her face balled up until she saw it was me, and she relaxed a little. "Dream tell this muthafucka to let me through! Ms. Rachel is still in there!" she was screaming and acting so crazy that it didn't register right away what she meant, but when it did, I took off running around the officer who still had his hands full trying to keep Destiny back. Despite the head start, I still managed to get stopped by another officer just as I made it over to the sidewalk. Salty tears filled my face as I broke down inside of his arms.

"Ma'am, calm down!"

"Pleeeeeeease, help Ms. Rachellll!" I continued to wail. My vision was blurry, as I gazed over at our burning business. I was having a complete meltdown and when I spotted one of the firefighters coming out of the building carrying what looked like a body I damn near fainted. He was already heading towards one of the ambulances on the scene when Elijah's voice boomed loudly over everything else.

"IS THAT MY FUCKIN MAMA!"

It seemed like a dozen officers were trying to stop him from getting to the ambulance, and they were either being knocked out of the way or getting dragged along behind him since his stride never broke. My heart shattered for him knowing that if anything happened to his mother, he'd be more than distraught. He was damn near at the ambulance door when they decided to tase him, but even as his body was struck with a high voltage of electricity, he still wouldn't drop. I knew that next they'd be trying to shoot him for his irate behavior, and honestly, I was surprised that none of them had yet to pull a gun. The officer that was restraining me let me go so that he could help with the bigger threat that was Elijah, and the moment he released me, I was right behind him. As police surrounded him barking out different orders, Elijah finally dropped to his knees from weakness.

"Stop resisting!" the one with the taser yelled, still releasing shocks to his body.

I broke through the barricade that they'd created around him, with fear radiating through my body. "Stop! Can't you see he's down, he ain't fuckin resisting no more!" I cried crouching in front of Elijah just as he fell over, exhausted from the struggle. Every bit of anger I had for him disappeared in that moment, and I quickly inspected him as his body convulsed.

"Ma-mmmmm." He struggled to speak, still trying to call out to Ms. Rachel.

"Please calm down Elijah, we're going to meet them at the hospital," I promised, with fresh tears falling from my eyes. "Get this shit out of him!"

An officer slowly approached brandishing a pair of cuffs, while the others moved in just a little more. It was obvious that they were scared as hell, they'd probably never seen someone fight this hard. But if they thought they were about to place him under arrest, they had me fucked up!

"I know you don't think you about to put those on him!"

"Ma'am, this is for his safety as well as ours-."

"You don't need to restrain him! He just wants to make sure his mother is okay! If yo ass pulled up to see your mother being dragged out of a burning building, wouldn't you be upset too?" I fumed looking around at all of them.

"Well...."

"Well, my ass! Take these fuckin' things out of him so we can go, because I promise if his mother doesn't make it and you've held him from seeing her we're gonna sue the shit outta y'all!" I could tell that he didn't like my tone or my attitude, but after looking at his co-workers, he finally put away the cuffs and bent to remove the prongs from Elijah's body.

Once they were out, I helped him into a sitting position as best I could, because he was just too damn heavy for me. Although he was still having a hard time speaking, the look in his eyes made it clear that he still had a nasty attitude with me, and that was further proven when he went to snatch away.

"You got some nerve trying to act funky with me after what you did, Elijah! Stop being an asshole and let me help get you to the hospital, and then you can do whatever the fuck you want!" I couldn't believe that he still wanted to be mad at me during a time like this, but if it was one thing I could do, it was match energy! Like I said I'd help his evil ass to the hospital and we could go right back to not talking to each other. I had way too much shit going on to deal with his bullshit, and that was a fact.

He shot me an evil look but didn't resist when I went to help him up again. By the time we got him to his feet and were making our way to my car, we were joined by Destiny and Juice who'd just arrived.

"What the fuck happened?" he asked, helping me to get Elijah into the front seat.

"I don't know! We closed up like normal, and Ms. Rachel said she'd lock up. I was damn near home when the alarm company called talkin' about the door had been broken! I tried to call her thinkin' that maybe she'd accidentally set it off, but she wouldn't answer and by the time I got back all of this was going on-!"

"Wait my OG in there!" a mixture of fear and anger washed over his face, and he started back towards the chaos, but Destiny pulled him back.

"Nooo they pulled her out a few minutes ago, and she's on her way to the hospital!" she cried frantically yanking his arm. I was already behind the wheel when they both jumped into the backseat. While we drove, Destiny filled us in on what the police and firefighters had been able to tell her, and it wasn't good. They'd found Ms. Rachel holed up in the back office, passed out from smoke inhalation. From what they'd said someone must have broken in and in an attempt to save herself she'd run into our office. The fact that they'd only come in to set the fire struck fear in me, and my stomach turned as Budda came to mind. He'd been sending me all types of threatening messages, and suddenly, our shop gets broken into and burned down. I couldn't imagine how afraid Ms. Rachel must have been having to go through what she had, and I found myself silently praying as I drove us to the nearest hospital.

Elijah who'd recovered during the drive was the first one to hop out once I pulled into the emergency room parking lot followed closely by Juice. I barely had time to take the damn key out of the ignition so that Destiny and I could catch up. When I did finally enter the emergency room both of them were at the desk scaring the shit out of the nurse there, demanding answers on where their mother was.

"Sir, I need you to calm down-."

"Bitch, I don't gotta do shit! Find my fuckin mama, before I tear all this shit up!" Elijah angrily pounded his fist against the desk, causing the poor lady to jump.

"Umm, I'm sorry we're looking for Rachel King, she was just brought in by ambulance." I quickly cut in trying to diffuse the situation before he made good on his threat or she called the police. She seemed genuinely happy to talk to someone that seemed sane, and she gave me a grateful look, avoiding eye contact with Elijah who stood there staring her down.

"O-okay, I'll see what I can find out."

"Don't see bitch *do!*" he ordered, and I cut my eyes at him, hoping to silence his mean ass, but he was trained on her. Nervously she glanced back and forth between the two of us before hurrying to type something into the computer.

"There's no word on her right now. She's still back with the doctors." Her voice trailed off as she focused back on us, clearly afraid of Elijah's reaction to her news. She was right to be scared with the way his eyes grew dark.

"Let's just wait and see what they say when they come out," I suggested lowly. He was already a ticking time bomb and wasn't really fucking with me, but I had to try. If his anger boiled over, there was no telling what he'd do, and he'd already just had an episode with the police not even an hour before. I took a chance and placed my hand on top of his where it rested on top of the desk, making him turn his gaze my way.

"Yeah come on bro," Juice agreed with a hand on his shoulder. Snatching away with a frustrated growl, he walked off to where they had chairs set up in the corner. Despite our issues, I felt terrible for him. Not too long ago, we were dealing with almost the same thing, and waiting to find out the fate of a loved one. The fact that it was their mother this time was for sure weighing heavily on him, and even more on me because I feared that I was the reason this happened. Just looking with his shoulders slumped in defeat had my eyes brimming with a fresh set of tears.

We all made our way over to the empty chairs, taking a seat to await whatever news the doctor would be bringing out, while Elijah paced the floor. Ten minutes later, Mr. King arrived with Yo'Sahn in tow and instantly wrapped his sons up into tight hugs. He was obviously distraught from the news as he broke down crying, damn near having to be held up by them. Once again, Destiny told the story of what happened while Yoshi buried his face into her chest. We all loved Ms. Rachel, and anything happening to her would destroy us.

It felt like hours later before a doctor finally emerged from the back and my chest tightened as he called us over. The expression on his face was grim, and before he even said anything, I knew it wouldn't be good news. "Family of Rachel King?"

"We're here. Please tell me my wife is okay." Mr. King was the first one to reach him, hopefulness in his tone.

"I'm sorry, we tried everything we could, but the damage to her lungs was just too extensive. Mrs. King suffered cardiac arrest while on the table, and after multiple attempts to revive her, we were unsuccessful."

"No! Take yo ass back there and get my OG dog!" Juice barked stepping into the doctor's face and shoving him backwards.

"Jeremiah!" his father grabbed him up, allowing the doctor to escape while Elijah angrily tore up the waiting room. There was so much going on at once that I didn't notice Destiny had fainted until I heard Yo'Sahn screaming her name in terror.

DESTINY

$\mathcal{I}$ woke up squinting at the bright ass light that bathed the room and immediately wished I could close my eyes right back as flashbacks hit me. Not only had our business burned down, but Ms. Rachel was dead. My mind didn't want to allow me to accept that shit. I *couldn't* accept that the lady who'd befriended and taken a chance on us was no longer alive.

A whimper fell from my lips, and I became overcome with emotion, causing Dream to run over to me frantically. "Oh my god, are you okay!" she asked, pulling me into a hug and showering me with kisses. I nodded, unable to form any words as I tried to swallow back my tears even though I was far from okay. In a way, I felt like all of this was my fault. I should've never left her alone. It wasn't our regular routine to have her still be there that late. She'd let one of her close friends schedule an appointment a couple of hours before closing time. It was a simple curl set and hadn't even taken very long. Ms. Rachel was finished and cleaning around her station when she suggested she lock up. Honestly, I wasn't feeling good and was supposed to have Jaceon over, so I jumped at the chance to leave a half-hour earlier, but now I was regretting it. Maybe if I had stayed, none of this would have happened.

"Girl, you scared the fuck outta me!" she fussed wiping her face. "Yoshi was so worked up one of the nurses had to take him into a different room so he could calm down!" I could almost see her heart pounding out of her chest from my passing out, but I didn't even know what had happened. One minute I was standing there holding on to Yo'Sahn and the next I was falling on that hard ass floor.

"Where is everyone else? Juice?" even though I was still feeling a little foggy and dealing with my own sadness I knew that losing his mother was going to have Juice going crazy if it hadn't already.

"After checking on Ms. Rachel, and hearing that you were okay they......left." She shrugged, looking off to the side. We both knew exactly what they were going to go do and I was sure that the city wasn't prepared. "Speaking of which, nobody's been back in here since they hooked you up to this IV and took your blood." I looked down at the IV in my arm and frowned. I hadn't even realized that I had one in me this whole time.

"What the fu-."

A knock sounded at the door and in stepped an older white man dressed in blue scrubs. "Hi, I'm Dr Spencer." He reached out to shake my hand, and I weakly gave it to him, surprised by how warm his was. "Now you fainted after hearing some bad news, I heard."

My cheeks warmed, and once again a reminder of what had happened with Ms. Rachel had me ready to cry again as I nodded. "Yeah...I-."

"It's actually more common than you think trust me, but in addition to that you were a little dehydrated, and you also have a bit of good news to counteract the bad." I guess he paused for dramatic effect or something, but when I looked at him blankly, he let out a chuckle and continued. "You're about six weeks pregnant, give or take. Congratulations!"

"No, the fuck I ain't!" I blurted, shaking my head emphatically. My reaction must have caught him off guard because the smile he had on his face fell and he glanced over at Dream before looking back at me.

"Oh..well, um...I'm pretty sure that you are, and it's natural to be afraid-."

"I'm not afraid. I'm mad as hell!" I glared at him like he was the reason I was pregnant before burying my face in my hands. This was too much. It seemed like every time I turned around, something else was going wrong, and now I was pregnant. There was really no telling how Juice was going to take this especially since they were still trying to figure out who shot him, and now who had been dumb enough to kill their mama. Dream rubbed my back and tried to tell me that things would be okay, but that shit wasn't helping, especially since she sounded happy about it.

"Okay, so since you've finished your IV I'll go ahead and get your paperwork ready." He talked quickly and rushed out of the room.

"Ooooh bitch, I knew it was a reason you around here fainting like a damn white woman." Dream said as soon as the door closed behind him.

I lifted my head and gave her a dry look. "Really Dream?" I knew it was her attempt at lightening the mood, but it was really a bad time. My mind was still trying to process Ms. Rachel's death and the announcement of a damn baby.

"Sorry," she shrugged. "But I did try to tell you."

"Ma!" Yo'Sahn ran into the room followed by a nurse carrying discharge papers. I shot Dream a look over his shoulder as I hugged him, so she knew not to say anything. My baby had been through enough today, and I didn't want to add to his stress, especially considering that I wasn't sure whether I was keeping it or not. "Are you okay?"

"Yeah I'm fine, I promise," I told him kissing his face. I could feel his body relax once I said that making me feel even worse. He was probably terrified having me pass out after hearing about Ms. Rachel. Which was further proven by how close he stuck by my side, even as the nurse removed my IV and had me sign my papers for release. She started to give me some basic care instructions, but I quickly put a stop to that shit, knowing that they'd involve something about this baby.

It didn't take long, and we were out the door heading home. Yo'Sahn was asleep within fifteen minutes of the drive, and instead of having Dream drop us off at my car, I just had her take us home. I had a lot of shit to think about, and I was already dreading tomorrow.

"Girl, who the hell is that?" Dream's voice brought me out of my reverie, and I realized that we'd already pulled up to my house and somebody was sitting on the steps. I peered out of the window trying to get a good look at whoever it was, but I could barely see since it was so dark.

"I don't know." I frowned.

"Should I pull off? I'm bouta pull off!" Dream's scary ass went to put the car in drive, just as whoever it was came down off the porch and I realized it was Jaceon.

"It's cool its just JC." Sighing I prepared myself for the bull-shit he was about to come with judging from the scowl on his face as he walked down to the car.

"Okay, well call me in the morning. We still need to talk to the police and figure out what to do about the business." She said, eyeing him suspiciously. I promised to do so and shook Yo'Sahn awake, before getting out myself trying my hardest to ignore the nigga standing on the sidewalk waiting for me. Of all the problems that me being pregnant by Juice would bring Jaceon happened to be the one that slipped my damn mind. I figured I didn't have to tell him anything yet anyway, because I wasn't sure if I was even going to keep it. I tried to tell myself that as I sent Yo'Sahn in ahead of us. Thankfully, despite the murderous look on his face Jaceon had enough sense to wait until we'd entered my bedroom and closed the door before he started in on me.

"Where you been Destiny? I been calling you for hours-, I thought you were hurt or something." He hissed as I set the papers and my keys on top of my dresser. "I bet you were with that nigga Juice right? That's the only time yo ass don't answer the phone!"

With my back to him, I began to find me something to sleep in as I tried to tame my growing anger. I was more than a little fed up with his constant accusations. It was understandable for him to be concerned about not reaching me, but bringing up Juice was doing too much.

"You need to lower your fucking voice, while my son in the next room sleeping!" I shot back, snatching a long t-shirt out of my dresser and slamming it closed despite what I'd just told him about Yo'Sahn being asleep.

"So you just gone skip right on over my question and shit? I guess that tells me everything I need to know right?" he chuckled bitterly, massaging his temples like I was trying his patience.

"You know what I really don't care what it tells you, but if you must know I been at the hospital! Not only did our salon get set on fire, but Ms. Rachel died tonight! So, yes I was with Juice, but not how you think." Another wave of emotion had me tearing up, and his face instantly softened, as he took a step toward me, but it was too late for that.

"Damn, my bad-."

"Yeah, it is yo bad." I sneered looking him up and down. "I think you should go." With my lips set in a grim line, I folded my arms. A part of me knew that I was using this argument to get rid of him, but at the moment, I didn't care. He was getting on my already frazzled nerves, and I just wanted to be alone to calm my mind.

"Destiny-." He started, but I held up a hand to stop him.

"Nah for real, I can't deal with this shit tonight."

His shoulders slumped in defeat, and he wet his lips before sighing. "Ayite, I'll just check up on you tomorrow?" he asked in hesitation, planting a kiss on my cheek once I nodded my agreement. "okay, cool, and I'm for real, sorry about the shop and Ms. Rachel." I barely acknowledged his weak ass apology as he turned and left. I didn't move until I heard the front door close and went to check the locks behind him. After everything that I had been through with Dre, I was dealing with the same type of shit, and the only difference was that he was financially stable. Regardless of the reasons I'd been staying with Jaceon, I knew that I no longer wanted to deal with his tantrums and I wasn't going to. I just needed to let him know that sooner rather than later.

EAZY

"You want something to eat baby?" my Aunt Stacey asked, holding out a plate packed high with greens, cornbread, baked macaroni, sweet potatoes and damn near a whole roast. She knew everything that I liked, so she'd already loaded it up, but I didn't have an appetite.

"Nah, I'm good Aunty," I said dryly, taking her in behind my dark shades. The hopeful look she wore quickly dropped, and she nodded her head in understanding, giving my arm a little squeeze. I was glad when she finally walked off. Looking at her was like staring in the face of my mama since they favored so much, and it wasn't doing shit but adding to my already fucked up mood. I wanted to be left alone. All of our family was there, filling up my parent's house and crying. They'd come to pay their respects, but after being stopped for the fiftieth time for a tearful hug and encouraging words I ducked off in a corner alone, hoping not to be bothered again.

My mother's home-going was beautiful, only the best just like she deserved. She had an ivory casket lined in gold, with the softest silk inside. Pops had picked out a white, chiffon dress from Dior for her and it made her look angelic and peaceful.

We'd had the church decorated with pink roses and the family all had one pinned to them. When I say the church was packed, I meant that! There were so many people that my mama had touched and befriended that there wasn't room for everyone. That didn't stop them from standing along the walls and the back of the church just so that they could be a part of her home-going. After a long service and the releasing of doves, we had her carried to the burial site by horse-drawn carriage. I'd kept my shades on the whole time unable to meet the eyes of my pops. He hadn't said anything or even acted as if he blamed me, but I felt it in my heart that he did. How could he not? Besides the issues that me and Juice had created, there'd been none in their lives. My pops was burying his better half, and it was because of our bullshit.

Despite the sadness surrounding him today, he'd kept it together for the most part, shedding his tears silently and trying to remain strong for us. Still, I knew that he was dying on the inside no matter what he said or how well he was keeping it together. Juice was just as stoic as me though, only speaking when spoken to but obviously wanting to be left alone.

Yo'Sahn was hanging close to my pops, wanting to be next to the person that had the strongest connection to Rachel King. They'd become his surrogate grandparents in a way, and he was just as hurt as everyone if not more so. It was like he'd just gained another person in his life that cared for him only to lose her suddenly. I felt for him, but I also couldn't get past my own issues with the matter.

These were all of the things on my mind at the moment, so when I saw my messy ass cousin Deidra aka Dee Dee walking my way I sighed. I already didn't really want to talk to anybody, but the loud mouth of the family was sure to piss me off. She sat down next to me, assaulting my nose with whatever strong ass perfume she was wearing.

"Hey cuz!" She gushed. "How you holdin' up?"

"I'm straight." I figured if I kept it short, she'd move on just like everyone else had, but she just made herself more comfortable touching my shoulder in consolation.

"I'm sorry about aunt Rachel, you know she was my favorite. She wasn't stuck up like some of these bitches in here." Her voice dropped to avoid anybody besides me hearing her.

I took a deep breath and tried not to snap. "What you want, Dee Dee?"

Shocked by my tone, her mouth dropped open, but she quickly recovered, clearing her throat before getting to the actual reason she was bothering me. "Wellll, I was just wondering if you could put my baby daddy, Lamar, on? He just got out and-."

"Yo is you fuckin crazy!" I growled jumping to my feet, causing her to wince and stand also.

"I just-."

"And you still talking? Get the fuck away from me bitch fore I kill yo ass in here!" I didn't even realize it, but I'd grabbed her ass by the throat and was squeezing as I spoke to her. Screams and cries of alarm sounded around us, but I kept my focus on her, as she gasped and clawed at my hand.

"Elijah!" my pop's voice thundered over everyone else's. He pushed his way through and came to a stop by my side. "Let her go, son." As angry as I was, my father's order had me releasing her dumb ass. My aunts and cousins hurried to usher her away while she sputtered and tried to suck in as much air as possible. They thought that I was just upset, but I was really ready to choke her ass to death right in my mama's dining room. I stood there for a minute, trying to calm down as my father watched me closely.

"I'm cool man." I finally said, hoping that he would carry on like everyone else had, but he didn't budge.

"Elijah-."

"I said I'm cool!" The fact that I was snapping at him when

he wasn't the one I was mad at fucked me up, but that didn't stop me from leaving him standing right there. I just needed a minute to myself, and then I'd come and apologize. A wide girth was made for me as I stormed off towards the back door, to get some air, and that was fine with me. As soon as I opened the door and stepped out onto the deck, thick weed smoke filled my nostrils. Juice sitting down at the table out there didn't surprise me at all. We were a lot alike, needing to grieve in our own time and in our own way. His way just happened to be smoking a blunt out behind the house where no one else was.

"I should've known yo ass was out here." I chuckled dryly, taking a seat across from him and accepting the half of blunt he held out to me.

He shrugged and cracked a small smirk. "Shit aunt Stacey ass was in there tryna shove food down my throat and shit, between her and aunt Janet I had to get away. What Dee Dee ass say to have you choking her out in there?"

"Slow ass bitch asked me about puttin' her baby daddy on! Goofy shit!"

"See she knew better than to come askin' me some dumb shit like that. I would've shot her ass in the foot tryna play with me." He huffed. "That's why she came to you. Everybody thinks you're the nice one." I shook my head and handed him his blunt back releasing a cloud of smoke as I did.

"Well, now they know I'm not." There were things that I was still trying to work out for myself. I couldn't talk to my mama about it, and I wasn't fucking with Budda. It felt like the only person I had to talk to was Juice and we all know what type of advice he'd give. He'd literally just told me he would have shot our cousin in the foot, with a house full of witnesses. It wasn't like I hadn't just almost choked her out, but that wasn't normally how I acted.

He silently agreed with a head nod, and we spent the next few minutes in silence, just passing his blunt back and forth until it was gone. The potent weed had done the trick, and I was in a much calmer state than I'd been before I came out there.

"I'm bouta go get me a drink. You want one?" He asked after tossing the duck.

"Yeah, gone head get me some D'usse." Nodding, he walked off and headed inside, leaving me alone for a minute. I was enjoying the breeze and the quiet, so much so, that I didn't even realize Dream had come out until she stepped into view. I'd seen her when she'd first walked into the church, distracting me and every other nigga in there with a pulse. The black dress that she'd decided to wear fit her like a glove and stopped just above her calves showing off her thick body. I took her in from the curls dancing around her head to the sliver of cleavage she had exposed and all the way down to her black, high heels. Her eyes were red and glossy from how much she'd been crying today, but she was still gorgeous.

I didn't know what the fuck Juice's ass had in that weed, but the usual anger I felt at the sight of her wasn't there. Unlike when any of my relatives had approached me, her presence didn't immediately make me want to go off, and I realized it was because I actually wanted her there. We stared at each other for a minute, neither of us saying anything, although I know she'd brought her ass out there for a reason.

She inched her way closer, stopping a few feet away before asking. "Are you okay?"

"Shiiiit, as okay as I can be considering." I shrugged, with low eyes that had me resting my head back just so I could see her. She looked good enough to make me forget why I was even mad at her in the first place, but despite that and me wanting to be alone with her my pride wouldn't let me say what I really wanted to. I really wanted to ask her how she'd been, pull her into my arms and hold her close to me, but pride is a mutha-fucka! So, instead of doing that I looked out into the yard, seemingly done with whatever conversation we could have had.

Dream being the type of woman she was stood there…waiting until she became fed up.

"You know what, fuck you *Eazy*! You can't swallow yo pride long enough to have an adult conversation with me, on a day when we're BOTH hurting! This is the second time that I've tried to be there for you when you know you don't deserve it, and you just keep giving me yo ass to kiss! Well, you don't have to EVER worry about me speaking to yo ass again! Trust me!" she was going off, rolling her neck and wagging her damn finger at me. Something in the way she spoke let me know that she was serious when she said it, unlike the previous times and my chest tightened. I don't know why I expected for her to give me so many chances to get my shit together, but that's just how niggas were. Even now as she basically told me she was giving up I still couldn't fix my lips to stop her.

"What the fuck going on out here?"

I immediately squeezed my eyes shut and blew air out of my mouth when Sherice's annoying ass stepped outside with us. I don't know how she found out anything about my mama's funeral, because I damn sure didn't tell her.

"Sherice, now ain't the time girl, I'm not tryna beat yo ass today." Dream chuckled, but the warning in her tone still didn't stop Sherice.

"I'm not at all surprised that you'd try to fight me at a repast, you've always been so… ghetto. No wonder Elijah came back to me, that ratchet shit can only get you so far."

"Aye man-." I tried to cut in, but Dream wasn't having it.

"Oh, so fucking with five different niggas at the same time ain't ratchet? That business that I RAN for you don't make you better than me, but if he wants you after what you did to him then so be it! You can have his ass!" she snapped rushing Sherice and mushing her. I jumped out of my seat, to try and stop them from brawling, but instead of retaliating Sherice just stood there rubbing her forehead while Dream stormed off. I hadn't realized it, but my whole damn family had heard the commotion and come out to watch the drama, with Destiny and Juice right in front.

"Elijah, you're just going to stand there?" Sherice shrieked like she'd really been hurt. I grit my teeth, already fed up with her bullshit for the day. "She could've hurt our baby, and you just gone let that shit slide?"

"Oh, hell naw, see now you trying me hoe and I ain't shit like my sister I'll mop this deck with yo ass!" Destiny flew over and was in her face before I could even react. With the precision of a boxer, she hit Sherice with a combo so vicious that she just dropped to the ground knocked out cold.

"And you nigga! I been tryna be quiet about this whole thing, but you really doing too much now. Did my sister go see Budda against my advice? Yes! But she went to tell him to leave her alone! That nigga been abusing her and some more shit, and she ain't had no contact with him this entire time! But she felt that she needed to let him know she was with you and she loved yo dumb ass and this is how you treat her! I swear to God she better than me cause I'd have cut yo ass if I was her. Now you and yo drama done fucked up our celebration of Ms. Rachel! You lucky I'm pregnant, or I'd tear all this shit up!"

"Pregnant?" Juice's voice sounded, while Destiny rolled her eyes and huffed.

"Aww shit. You just around here fuckin everything up!"

Juice snatched her ass up and dragged her into the house leaving me to think on everything that she'd just told me about her sister.

JUICE

*A*fter having to bury my mama, the last thing I expected to go down was Eazy choking out our cousin and Destiny beating Sherice's ass. Though it was all entertaining, finding out that Destiny was pregnant sobered me right the fuck up! I mean as a grown ass man I knew the repercussions of going in raw, I'd avoided the shit since I'd been fucking just so I wouldn't get caught up and look at me now. It wasn't a terrible thing getting a woman like Destiny pregnant, cause she was a good ass mama, the problem was whether or not the baby was mine. She called herself talking to some new nigga, and before me there was Dre, so I really didn't know what to think. Real shit, I was ready to kill her little short ass, so when I got her in the house, I demanded she get her shit ready because we needed to talk away from my nosy ass family.

After checking on my pops and Yo'Sahn who'd decided to stay, we left, and now I just kept stealing glances at her ass as we drove. She hadn't said shit since we got in the car, besides leaving numerous voicemails on Dream's phone trying to find out where she was. I knew that she was worried, but we had bigger issues to worry about at the moment. Dream was a grown ass woman, and although my brother was fucked up, they'd get their shit together eventually, but we had a baby to discuss.

"So, you really wasn't gone say shit?" I asked after she tried to call her sister for the hundredth time with no answer. She was avoiding the elephant in the car, and I wasn't about to keep playing with her.

She sucked her teeth like I was getting on her nerves. "What you mean?"

"Aye, Dream stop fuckin playin' with me! I'll pull this bitch over right now!" I glared her way with flared nostrils. She was playing games, but I wasn't above parking real quick and hemming her up until she told me what I wanted to know.

"Ugh fine! Yes, I was gonna say something… eventually." She admitted folding her arms.

"When, when you was too big to hide it! How long have you known Destiny?"

"I found out at the hospital….the day Ms. Rachel died. I was waiting for the right time. I'm still not even sure I wanna keep it." It was a good thing we'd finally made it to her crib because I would've wrecked after her saying some goofy-ass shit like that. I stomped on the brakes so hard she almost hit the dash. "Nigga are you crazy!"

"You lucky I ain't just shoot yo dumb ass, don't fuckin play with me! If that's my baby, you definitely keeping it!" I beat death only to lose my mother right after, and now she was trying to tell me that she would kill my damn baby! That shit wasn't happening, and I didn't care if I wasn't ready to be a father. The death of Rachel King had fucked me up, and I was ready to get on some reckless shit, not caring whether I lived or died. Hearing that Destiny was pregnant and knowing it could be mine though was like my OG talking to me from the grave and telling me that I needed to be here for Yo'Sahn and now this baby. Destiny's mouth dropped open, and she slapped the shit out of me.

"What the fuck you mean *if!* Yo funny looking ass the only one I been fuckin! That's exactly the reason why I ain't sure about keeping it in the first place! I already got one shitty baby daddy, I don't need another one!" she was fuming mad with her heavy-handed ass, and I had to resist the urge to slap her back as she hopped out of the car slamming my door in the process.

"Aye bring yo ass back here Destiny!" I barked getting out just as she crossed the street, switching hard as hell in the form-fitting dress she was wearing.

"Kiss my ass nigga!"

"I'm gone kiss that muhfucka alright." Grumbling I followed behind her ready to break my foot off in her ass. "If yo dumb ass trip and hurt that baby tryna be mad I'm gone fuck you up!"

She raised her middle finger high and started working her hips harder, with her heels clacking loudly as she walked. I was already pissed off, but the sight of her so-called nigga walking down from her porch had me in a full rage. She seemed shocked by his presence and instantly backed up.

"Yo you pregnant by this nigga!" he sneered, walking up on her. "I knew this shit, you been fuckin his ass this whole time and tryna act like you a good girl and shit! Got me out here like a goofy tryna wine and dine yo slut ass!"

I finally made it over to where they stood since my slight limp slowed me down and gently moved her out of the way as she tried to explain herself to him. He didn't even get a chance to say whatever smart shit he was thinking because I rocked his jaw, hearing the crack of his teeth upon impact. Destiny screamed when he hit the ground holding his face, but I didn't let up. Grabbing him by his t-shirt, I lifted him up and hit him over and over until blood covered his face.

"Juice! Juice stop, he's not even fighting back!" Destiny was crying at this point as she tried to pull me off of him, only making things worse. I had a lot of pent up anger inside. I'd buried the woman who'd raised me today, and then I found out that I might be a father, and this nigga thought he could bring his tender dick ass over here talking crazy to my baby mama! I could understand that she was scared, but her best bet was to leave me the fuck alone until I was finished.

"Fuck off me D, take yo ass in the house!" I shrugged her off and stood up just so I could kick his ass wherever my feet landed.

"No! Cause I'm definitely not keeping this baby if you go to prison for killing him out here!" It was like she knew telling me that would stop the assault. I delivered one final kick to his stomach, and backed off, chest heaving as I glared at Destiny. She visibly released a sigh of relief, not giving a single fuck about the way I was eyeballing her.

Dude groaned from the ground letting us know that he wasn't dead, but his ass would need some serious dental work. Fucking around with Destiny I was out here trying to kill niggas with my bare hands.

"Get yo bitch ass up," I ordered clutching my side as I started to feel the effects of fighting after being shot up, I'd probably torn some stitches, but it wasn't like he didn't deserve it. JC struggled to his feet and limped off to wherever the fuck he came from, and I watched him until he disappeared from the block.

"I can't fuckin believe you!" she finally spoke once he was gone.

"Well believe it, and while you at it pack a bag. You comin' home with me." I told her unmoved by her attitude.

"Boy, boom! I ain't going nowhere with you!"

Sighing, I took a step in her direction and winced as pain shot through my stomach, stopping me in my tracks. "Shit!"

"Oh, my God! Are you okay!" her voice elevated in concern

she closed the distance between us and tried to look me over like her ass was a nurse and knew what she was doing.

"Fuck no." I gritted through clenched teeth.

"Good! Serves yo mean ass right! I'll go get some clothes, but we going to the hospital before we go to your house. You can wait in the car." She didn't even give me a chance to argue before she switched away, leaving me out there alone.

۶۰

SOME DAYS LATER I SAT IN THE CAR WITH EAZY SHARING A BLUNT. I'd been right the night of my mama's funeral my ass had needed stitches, in my shoulder and in my stomach. The whole two hours they'd had me in the emergency room me and Destiny argued like an old married couple, gaining looks from the nurses and even the doctor. They thought that shit was cute, up in there tryna make us couple goals and we weren't even a couple, but we would be and soon. I wasn't about to keep playing with Destiny. The baby was a sign that we were supposed to be together, despite what she'd been talking about before I was laying claim to her. That's what me beating dude's ass meant and that's what her keeping our baby meant too.

"It's time," Eazy said, breaking me out of my thoughts. After smashing my blunt out in the ashtray, I checked the gun on my waist and got out of the car. It was late, and surprisingly the block was empty, which made it easier for us to make our way down to the house without being seen. My adrenaline was rushing the closer we got and knowing what we were about to do.

We stepped onto the back porch as quietly as possible, and Eazy pulled out his tools to crack open the door. He hadn't broken into anything in so long I wondered if his ass even remembered what to do, but not even a minute later he had the door open, and we were creeping inside. The kitchen floor creaked under our weight, and we paused to make sure that we hadn't woken anybody up. After waiting a second without hearing any movement we ventured further inside, checking each bedroom along the way. They all came up empty, but the closer we got to the front of the house we could hear a t.v. playing softly. Eazy pointed at the closed door and started making hand signals like he was in the fucking army or some shit. I just waved his ass on and twisted the knob to let us in. As soon as we crossed the threshold, I could make out a body in the bed wrapped up in a thick blanket.

"Get yo ass up granny!" I hissed kicking the bed and making her stir, but not come out from under the cover.

"Really nigga?"

"What you want me to wake her up with breakfast or some shit, her ass bouta die muhfucka. It don't matter how she wakes up!" I kicked the bed again, this time snatching the covers off too, instantly causing the woman to jump into a sitting position.

"Ahhhh! What you doin' in my house!" she screamed looking between Eazy and me in fear. "If you lookin' for money I-I have some jewelry! Just take what you want and leave!"

"Don't nobody want that fake ass costume jewelry!" looking at her in disdain I came around to the side of the bed, while Eazy went to the other side and she backed into the headboard.

"I know who you are!" she gasped pointing a shaky finger at me. We hadn't worn any masks, so she could clearly see my face, and I made sure to smirk at her evilly.

"Good, then you know what I'm capable of! Where yo bitch ass grandson at?" I got right to the point pushing my gun against her temple. I knew that Dre was still alive, and I was betting that her old ass did too. She was going around talking to the police and dropping names when she knew that nigga wasn't dead. Tears instantly started raining down her sunken in face, but they didn't move me at all.

That nigga had tried to kill Yo'Sahn and me and if I had to

kill everybody that he held near and dear to him until he brought his bitch ass out of hiding, then I would. Starting with this old bitch. It wasn't how we usually got down, I was reckless, but I wasn't "kill women and children" reckless. However, I'd lost so much at this point that I didn't even care.

"Please, I-I."

"Where the fuck is Dre!" Eazy who'd been calm and cool this entire time finally spoke, obviously growing tired of the games.

"I don't knowwwww!" She wailed trembling so hard that my gun slipped. "I ain't spoke to him in at least a week! Last I heard he was with his cousin Brian at some lil hoes house!" Eazy and I shared a confused look. Out of all the things we knew about Dre we hadn't heard of him having a cousin named Brian. It was a family full of females from what we'd heard, where did a nigga named Brian come from?

"Who the fuck is that?" we said at the same time.

"His cousin! Their dads are brothers, but they have different mamas and-."

"Man, we ain't ask you for y'all family history and shit!" She was telling us all of this like it would help us find him. I was ready to go ahead and shoot her ass just to get her to stop talking and crying so damn much, but Eazy hit me with a warning look.

"Look lady, do the nigga got like a nickname or something? Is he from here?" his tone didn't give away how agitated he really was, but I could tell by the way he clenched his jaw that he was just as ready to get this shit over with as me. He wasn't his normal self, but he was doing much better since finding out that Dream hadn't betrayed him like he'd assumed. I'm sure that was the only reason he hadn't come in shooting first and asking questions later, but it was only so much more of this back and forth shit I could take. The old lady looked about the room like she was trying to think before her eyes widened.

"Budda! That's his street name, I never liked it, but that's what they called him!" she shrieked eagerly nodding her head as she spoke. I hit her with two bullets to her temple silencing anything else she was going to say and shared a look with Eazy. It went without saying that this was a much bigger issue than we'd thought. The plus side was that when we'd find one we'd find the other, the problem with that was whether or not we'd find them before they made another move.

BUDDA

$\mathscr{I}$ laced my blunt with precision before licking and twisting it closed. I'd been paranoid as fuck since Dre's dumb ass had told me about what he did. Although he went against my orders and probably made us even bigger targets, I had to admit that I was happy that something good came out of it. Not only had he stopped Dream's money flow, but he'd inadvertently killed them niggas' mama. It was going to definitely knock them off their square, making things easier for me to take over. I'd just need to move up my plans.

Getting an army behind me that was willing to go against Eazy and Juice was proving to be much harder than I thought. It wasn't too many niggas out here that wanted to go to war with them, and since my team was mostly either locked up or dead because of me, I had to start over fresh. Dre had already killed the only inside that we had, by shooting Grim's ass, but he wasn't trustworthy enough in my book anyway. Just like Dre had said, if he'd turn on them, he'd turn on us. I only had three niggas in my corner right now, and that wasn't anywhere near enough to take them down. The uneven circumstances were making me consider returning agent Green's calls. I'd been avoiding doing so because I was tired of dealing with them, despite snitching out my whole team they'd still given me five years and I had nothing to show for it. In the time I was gone, Eazy had taken over and gotten all of the things that belonged to me. The nigga that I had shown the ropes to had come up in a major way, and it was only because of the time I'd been down. The only thing he hadn't been able to get his hands on was my connect, but despite not having access to Santos, he'd managed to blow up with coke so pure that everybody wanted to get their hands on it. The shit had me more than tight, but I'd figure out a way to get my spot back AND get his connect in the process. Sparking my blunt, I inhaled deeply letting the smoke fill my lungs before blowing it out through my nose.

"Dammit Budda, I told you not to smoke that shit in here! It stinks!" Olivia came in snapping and trying to fan away the thick smoke that had filled the room, quickly pissing me off. She was always nagging and shit, it was like a day couldn't go by without me having to beat her ass for her to shut up. All a nigga was doing was smoking to relieve my stress, and here she comes yelling and fucking up the mood. "You said it was going to be different and nothing has changed Budda! You're still hitting on me and smoking them premos like a crackhe-!" Her sentence was cut short when I leapt off the couch, punching her ass in the nose. She instantly dropped like a sack of potatoes, and I hovered over her damn near foaming at the mouth.

"Say that shit again! I'm not a fuckin crackhead bitch!" I barked kicking her in the stomach repeatedly, while she cried and begged me to stop. That was the problem with her, she always came fucking with me and then wanted to cry like it wasn't her fault I was beating her ass. I never had to deal with this shit when I was with Dream. She knew better than to say half the shit that Olivia let slip out of her mouth. I had her broken in, and all it took was a five-year bid to break my hold on her.

Out of breath, I left her there on the floor curled up in a ball and crying with her hands over her face. I was going to finish my blunt, but in my haste to get to her I'd thrown it somewhere and couldn't find it. Now I wanted to beat her ass for that shit too! Instead of laying hands on her, I tore up the living room in search of it, still coming up empty.

"See what the fuck you did! I oughta beat yo ass again!" I spat angrily. My eyes landed on her purse lying next to her, and I snatched it up. She had over $800 inside, and I took it all out, stuffing it down into the pocket of my jeans.

"Buddaaaaa! What you doing, that's the rent money!" she made a weak attempt at sitting up and trying to reach for it, but I slapped her hand away roughly.

"I look like I give a fuck! You should've left me alone!" Throwing her purse. I hit her right in the face and stormed off while she just sat there crying.

AFTER I'D SPENT A MAJORITY OF THE MONEY GETTING HIGH AND tricking off with a couple of hoes, I knew I finally stumbled back into the apartment. I was hoping I'd be able to get some sleep, but the second I walked in the living room I saw Dre on the couch crying like a bitch to Olivia's raccoon eyed ass. My eyes narrowed at the sight, trying to figure out what the fuck was going on.

"Baby!" Olivia jumped up to meet me, knowing that I was five seconds off from fucking her up. "Dre just found Ms. Taylor's body! They said she was shot twice in the head!" she was in my face blubbering like a fool and I couldn't stop focusing on the damage I'd done to her earlier. Her nose was clearly swollen and probably broken, and she was sporting two black eyes. I was so repulsed I turned away and looked to Dre for answers.

"Bro they killed Granny!" he told me tearfully.

"Nigga they who?" my forehead bunched, confused as hell in my high state. I was so fucked up that I could barely even feel the severity of the situation.

"Juice and Eazy! They killed my fuckin' granny, I know it was them!"

He was crying and shit like we weren't in the middle of a war. I moved Olivia out of my way and grabbed that nigga up by the front of his shirt. "You over here cryin" and shit like we ain't in a war! Man, shut yo bitch ass up! Is you tryna get back at them niggas or sit in here crying like a female!" Honestly I didn't really give a fuck about them killing our granny. She was a bitch anyway at least she was to me, but I was tired of this hiding and shit. It was time to take back my rightful spot on top. I just needed Dre to get his shit together.

"I'm tryna get em back!" he told me sniffling with his chest puffed out.

"Ayite then. Let's do it."

DESTINY

J was meeting with I'yanna today to talk about what was going to happen as far as the salon went. We'd been so messed up after Ms. Rachel's death and the fact that our business had burned down that we hadn't had time to think about insurance or rebuilding. So, when she reached out to me, I was surprised and instantly concerned. Ms. Rachel said that she had insurance on the building, however, I wasn't sure that it would extend to us since we were only leasing it from her. It was a lot to think about, especially considering that I'd given her my savings and now I had less than nothing if the insurance didn't come through.

Tears stung my eyes as I pulled up outside of the salon and saw the damage in broad daylight. It looked much worse than it did that night, and it hurt my heart to know that Ms. Rachel had gotten trapped in there. Just thinking about it had me emotional as fuck and I hurried to wipe my face as I'yanna stepped out of her car. Still sniffling, I climbed out as well and met her on the curb right by the crime scene tape.

"Hey, I'yanna." I greeted forcing myself to smile despite my deep disdain for this rude bitch.

"Dream." Her tone was dry like she would rather be anywhere than here right now when she was the one that had called me. "Well, I called you here because I spoke with the insurance adjustor. Unfortunately, there were a few issues that were brought up, the first being the fact that you were merely leasing the building from Mrs. King."

"Yeah, I know but-."

She held a hand up to stop me from continuing. "Please let me finish. Also, since this was arson, they are not obligated to pay out since the policy doesn't cover those types of-."

"Bitch are you serious!" I fumed shaking my head in disbelief. "You had me come all the way out here just to tell me that bullshit when you could've just said this shit on the phone!" The snide grin on her face vanished as I moved into her personal space. It seemed like every time I turned around, I was getting some bad news, and the fact that this bitch was finding humor in my pain had me ready to beat her ass out here.

"Just because Mrs. King had a soft spot for you and your sister doesn't mean anything to me. Ever since you both came around, it's been nothing but trouble, starting with you trying to steal her sons away. Now , suddenly a lady who hasn't had any problems since I've known her dies in a fire that someone set in her building." She cocked her head, looking just as mad as I felt. "You don't deserve to get your business rebuilt, and technically it's not yours yet anyway." Unable to control myself anymore, I lunged at her. I'd been getting fucked with more times than I could count, by her, Budda, Sherice and Elijah. I was always looking the other way and trying to avoid confrontation, but this bitch was going to get this work ta-day!

She was so caught off guard that she fell backwards, and I landed right on top of her throwing a punch on the side of her temple as she screamed and swung wildly. Before I could hit her again though, I was being pulled away.

"Aye, stop all that wild shit!" Elijah's voice had me fighting harder to be free from his hold.

"Let me the fuck go!" I fumed wiggling against him.

"Not until you calm down!" After struggling some more, I realized that it was pointless. Elijah was strong as hell, and I wasn't doing shit but making myself tired.

"I'm calm! Now let me down!" I stilled in his arms, and he placed me on my feet just like he promised, backing away right after so that I wouldn't swing on his ass too. He knew me well because that was exactly what I was going to do. I didn't even know what he was doing there, and I wished he wouldn't have come. People thought that I was such an easy target because of my sweet and professional nature, but I was quickly going to show them that I had hands, and I was starting with I'yanna.

"I hope you know I'm pressing charges! You just attacked me for no reason!" She stood up, screaming and waving her phone in the air. There wasn't even anything wrong with her besides her looking disheveled. If she wanted to call the police on me, I was going to give her a real reason to. I started in her direction again only for Elijah to grab my arm, stopping me. He gave me one of those chilling looks that warned me not to try him before making his way to I'yanna. By now she had her back to us as she looked down at her phone, so she didn't notice him until he'd snatched it away and slipped it into his pocket. He was talking to her in a tone so low that I couldn't make out what he was saying, but whatever it was, he had her undivided attention. His ass was probably trying to fuck her too, and I wasn't about to sit there while he scheduled a hookup or whatever the fuck he was doing. Rolling my eyes, I stalked to my car, talking shit under my breath the whole way.

"Dream!"

Him yelling my name had me quickening my pace. I didn't know what he wanted, and after the way he'd been acting, I didn't want to find out either. As far as I was concerned, he could kiss my entire ass!

"Dream I ain't playing with you!" Just that fast he whipped me around and had me pinned against my damn door with a murderous look on his face.

"Don't you need to go finish talking to yo little hoe? Why you fuckin with me!" I hissed fed up with the entire situation. At this point I just wanted to go home and try to figure out my next move. I no longer had a business or any money, and that was a big problem not only for me but for Destiny too. The last thing I was trying to do was sit here going at it with him of all people. Especially when I'yanna had already threatened me with the police. If they were on the way, then I definitely needed to get the fuck out of there, and Elijah needed to get the fuck out of my face.

"Would I be chasing you if I needed to talk to her! I just made sure she ain't call the police on yo crazy ass, the least you can do is talk to me for a minute." There was no question that he was telling and not asking me, so I glanced at my watch to start the time on his sixty seconds.

"Okay, one minute go ahead and say what you need to," I told him folding my arms impatiently and causing him to chuckle.

"You and I both know I wasn't being literal. We need way longer than one minute." Licking his lips, he leaned in closer, and his cologne quickly filled my nostrils, making my body betray me by the way it responded. He was looking a little rough with his hair uncut and his beard growing wildly yet I couldn't help but notice he was still as sexy as ever, if not more so. The grungy look was working for him, coupled with the cotton navy shorts and white fitted tee that had his muscles bulging it was hard for me not to want him. I looked off to the side to distract myself and noticed that I'yanna was long gone. At least I knew the part about him stopping her from calling the police was true. If they were coming, they would've already been here, and she would've been running around screaming like an idiot.

"Okaaaay." I dragged smacking my lips. His brows furrowed at my impatience but he was the one that had stopped ME to talk, and he was taking his sweet ass time doing so. I honestly felt like he didn't even deserve a second of my time after what he'd done. I was tired of giving him my energy only for him to shit on me.

"Fuck I look like talking to yo ass out here. Follow me to my crib." If I had my eyes closed, I would've sworn that I was talking to Juice, just from his tone and delivery alone. This wasn't the Elijah that I was used to, and I had to assume it was because of the things he was currently going through. There was something dark and cold in his eyes, and the part of me that still loved him wanted to fix whatever was wrong. The bigger part of me knew that I shouldn't, but I still agreed like a damn fool. Without a word, he walked off to where his truck was parked not too far from mine, while I watched trying to figure out what the hell had just happened.

When I finally slid behind the wheel and turned my key, he was pulling up beside me waiting, and I promptly waved his ass on. I shifted into drive as the sounds of Kehlani's *While We Wait* album started bumping through my speakers. The lyrics to the first song had me mulling over our situation, and all in my feels with how accurate it was. Elijah and I HAD moved too fast, and I thought the way he loved me would complete me. I put so much hope into him that it crushed me how easy it was for him to turn his back on me, and over an assumption at that. As I drove, thinking it over, I realized that my ass would be stupid as hell to even consider talking to him right now. He hadn't even apologized for the shit with Sherice, let alone allowed me to explain my side of the story. I was sure that the only reason he had any words for me right now was because of Destiny going off on him at Ms. Rachel's repast. She'd told me all about it and how she had beat Sherice's ass. I couldn't lie; I laughed hard despite how hurt I was over the betrayal. As crazy as it sounded I was so used to being cheated on that when I saw Elijah fucking Sherice in his office that day I couldn't even do shit. I wasn't expecting *him* to do that, but he had, and now he wanted me to give him something he hadn't even extended to me, which was a chance to explain. There wasn't anything he could say to me that would make me understand his logic so, when he took the left towards his apartment, I quickly took a right, barely avoiding a minivan that was coming the same way. The lady honked her horn, and I could tell she was cursing me out as I sped away.

I hadn't even gotten a block away, and my phone was lighting up with calls from Elijah, but I let it go to voicemail every time. Knowing that my house would be the first place he'd go to find me and Destiny's would be the second I went to my mama's house against my better judgement. It was the last place he would think to look considering that I'd told him about our strained relationship. I wasn't sure if she'd even be there considering her crazy ass hours, but when I pulled up to her building a half-hour later and saw her maroon Lumina parked out front relief washed over me briefly. At least I knew she was home, and now I just had to get her to actually let me in. As sad as it was our mama wasn't always too happy to see either of us, especially when it came to me. For whatever reason, she always seemed to like me a little less than Destiny, so when we were around each other, it never went well. The fact that I was even willing to come here to escape Elijah was significant because I couldn't stand my mama about ninety-nine percent of the time. Sighing at the lengths I was going through, to avoid this nigga I pulled away and made a trip to the liquor store around the corner. If nothing else got her to open the door, a fifth of Paul Masson would. I made sure to grab me some wine too because there was no way I'd be able to deal with my mama sober, especially if she'd be drinking herself.

With our drinks in hand, I hustled to her door ignoring the catcalls of a few niggas that were milling around and rang her buzzer. It took her forever to answer, and I could hear her attitude through the intercom when she did.

"Who the hell is it!"

"It's me….Dream." I said waiting for her to speak or buzz me in. After an uncomfortable pause, I went ahead and added. "I got you some, Paul." A second later, the buzzer sounded, and I pulled the door open rolling my eyes. My mama was a whole trip if I hadn't brought her a bottle she was going to act like she didn't even know I was out there.

As soon as she opened her door, she rolled her eyes and reached for the bag I was holding. "Well hey to you too ma," I grumbled following her inside.

"Girl don't be actin like you care about me speaking when you don't even call or visit. You must want something cause I can't even remember the last time you brought yo ass over here." She was right. I never visited, and it was mostly because of her stank ass attitude. She always had something smart to say, and my mouth could be just as flip as hers so we could never coexist in the same space for long. I was hoping though that this wouldn't be one of those times, because I literally had nowhere else to go.

"Me comin' over here don't automatically mean I want something….maybe I just wanted to check on you." I looked around as we walked through her cramped apartment. She still had the same red leather living room set that Budda had bought her years ago, even though it was all torn up. Even though she'd gotten evicted more than anybody I know she always made sure to keep her shit, no matter how outdated it was. She had a ton of knick-knacks that didn't go together all over the place, making her apartment look more like a thrift store than a place somebody lived. Her sixty-inch flat screen was nestled on a stack of crates, and I cringed just thinking about how easily it could fall off. Never mind the fact that the shit just looked tacky as fuck, but my mama didn't care about that. Her having a tv that big was good enough in her mind.

She stopped in the doorway to the kitchen and smacked her lips. "Bitch please, check on me my ass. Don't think I forgot about the way you treated me at yo shop with yo rude ass. You don't give a damn about checking on me. Now, what's the real reason you came over here?"

I took a seat on the couch, not bothering to follow her to the kitchen. The way she was already going off, I was ready to drink my shit straight out the bottle fuck a cup! "I'm not bouta argue with you. I really wanted to see you, but I can go home if you gone be acting like this." As much as I didn't want to I would definitely leave and go home. I wasn't trying to go back and forth with her. I was already going through enough. I started to get myself prepared to leave, not even waiting on her to reply.

"Sit yo ass down Dream! I swear you so dramatic!" She appeared in the doorway with two glasses in hand and our bottles. I was still standing as she came further in the room and sat on the couch opposite me. It wasn't until she had poured her a shot and pushed the other glass and my wine towards me that I actually sat down.

"I'm *not* dramatic," I grumbled with my back stiffened and poured myself a hefty glass. She raised her brow with a smirk before polishing off her drink, without bothering to comment which was just fine with me. The time I would be spending over here would go much smoother if she kept that same energy, but I knew that would be too much like right for her, which she proved a second later once she'd downed her second shot.

"Anyways, I heard about what happened to y'all lil salon." She said, and I winced at how callous she was being about it.

She always called it "little" like it wasn't a big endeavor for us. I took a deep breath and drank some more.

"Yeah that shit was messed up." I was trying to keep it short. I didn't really want to talk about that, not with her anyway. So instead of getting into an in-depth conversation about it, I put my attention on the crime show she'd been watching when I came in.

"I knew something like this was gone happen cause y'all ain't need a business no way. Now y'all done wasted all this time and money for nothing. You better hope you can get yo old job back cause I know y'all dumb asses ain't have no insurance, did you?" She challenged, making me want to spit my drink in her face. This was our mama, and she was calling us dumb and talking about our business like it was negative. She hadn't even said she was sorry about what had happened and I knew that was because she really didn't care. In fact, she was probably happy about us failing at anything outside of the norm.

"See, I knew I shouldn't have come over here." I spoke as I once again started gathering up my stuff. I'd just tried to fight a whole lawyer for the very same thing, and before I put my hands on my mother, I would remove myself from the situation even though she deserved to be punched in her mouth.

"Why, cause I told yo ass the truth! That's what I'm talkin bout! You mad cause I don't be tryna kiss yo ass like these other muhfuckas? Be mad then, I ain't call you over here no way!" She spat, leaning back into her seat and waving me off.

"No, I'm mad cause you're a shitty excuse for a mama! You ain't even said you were sorry about what happened to a business we saved and worked so hard for! But you got time to talk shit like you ever did anything with your life besides drink and pop that old ass pussy for niggas that didn't even bother to stay with your miserable ass!" I was over it as I twisted the cap back on my bottle while she just sat there opening and closing her mouth.

"Oh you can definitely get yo ass the fuck on talking bout my pussy old! Yous a foul mouth ungrateful lil bitch ugh!" She didn't need to tell me twice. I was already making my way to the door anyway, but I paused long enough to let her pass me. Anybody that would talk to a person that they had birthed the way she'd just spoken to me then it was no telling what she'd do. It was by the grace of God that I allowed her to bump me on her way to the door without me snatching her back by the draw-string ponytail she was wearing.

"Girl fuck you and this cramped ass apartment!" I said as soon as I crossed the threshold and was out in the hallway, only to be met with her door slamming in my face. This behavior wasn't anything new from her, but it never stopped it from hurting any less. It was just a part of life with her as our mama. Now I had to take my ass home and hope that I didn't see Elijah or better yet he'd better hope he didn't see ME with the way I was feeling!

EAZY

I was mad as hell that Dream had me looking for her ass after she said she'd meet me at my crib. I didn't even know how I'd lost her. She had to be driving like she was in Talladega nights or some shit to have gotten away so fast. As mad as I was that didn't stop me from circling the area before eventually heading to her apartment where her ass wasn't at blowing up her phone the whole time. A part of me wanted to just let it go for the day, but I'd already invested so much time into this shit that I couldn't let it slide. Especially since I found out about what really happened with Budda. I admit that I jumped the gun and acted stupid which wasn't like me, but in my defense, I'd just learned that my mentor the nigga I thought I could trust above everybody, even my brother was a fucking snitch! And not only that, but they used to have a relationship. That put the last nail in the proverbial coffin for me, and I really didn't need to hear shit she had to say. If I would've just waited instead of acting on impulse, then I would have found out the truth. Instead, I went ahead and fucked Sherice then let Dream catch me like an idiot.

Even after that she'd made multiple attempts to try and talk to me, but I wasn't trying to fuck with her. Now she ain't wanna have shit to do with my black ass, and I couldn't say that I blamed her, but as a man, I knew that I needed to apologize. I could always admit when I was wrong, and I definitely was in this instance. I'd found out that she would be at the shop today from I'yanna's secretary, so I made my way over there with hopes of talking things out with her and pulled up just in time to stop her from beating I'yanna's ass. I had to admit that she got a good couple of shots off on her and that shit was kind of sexy considering Dream's usually calm demeanor. Even though I wanted to see her dig in shorty's ass because I was sure I'yanna deserved it I still went ahead and put a stop to the fight. Then I made sure there wouldn't be any legal actions taken. I'yanna liked to pretend she was big and bad, but she knew to pipe down with that 911 shit when I pressed her. I thought that had gotten me an in with Dream, but her ass rushed up outta there. Now I couldn't find her. Frustrated, I drove away from her apartment knowing there was only a handful of places she could be.

"Hey Siri, call Juice." I barked stopping at a red light and drumming my fingers impatiently as I waited for her to connect the call.

"Aye Destiny you better sit yo pregnant ass down somewhere for real!" He spoke into the background before bringing his attention to me. "Wassup bro." I could hear Destiny going off faintly, but I couldn't make out what she was saying. Ever since she'd told us she was pregnant, he'd been on her ass heavy, and I didn't blame him. I was actually proud of the way he'd stepped up, and I knew our OG would be too. It was really fucked up that she wouldn't be around to see her only grandchild and I say only because it wasn't no way that Sherice was pregnant after I'd watched her swallow that damn plan B. She just said that shit to piss Dream off if she knew what was good for her though she'd stop playing with me. Had Destiny not laid her out I would've for trying to pull that bullshit. I still had yet to address her about it, however, every time she called, I was sending her straight to voicemail, but I planned on handling her as soon as I finished with Dream.

"Nigga, you called me just to breathe in my fuckin' ear or is you gone say something!" Juice huffed, snapping me out of my thoughts at the same time that a horn blew behind me.

"Shut yo ass up, I ain't Destiny muhfucka. I'll still beat yo ass! Fuck y'all over there arguing about already anyway?" I wanted to know. He'd told me how he had basically forced her and Yo'Sahn over to his house and refused to let them go back to theirs. I could only imagine how that had been working out for him so far. A pregnant Destiny and a preteen, all in his space was probably driving his evil ass crazy.

"Mannnn I'yanna was just blowing me up, so now she thinks we been conversating on the low."

"It's converse slow ass nigga and don't be telling him my business! I don't like his ass right now!" Destiny corrected him before I could, letting me know that he'd put me on speaker, probably for her benefit. Despite my current situation and the fact that she said she didn't like me, I couldn't help but laugh as they argued back and forth.

"Aye you like five minutes pregnant and you already acting up, keep playing with me, and ima put yo ass in a headlock for real!"

"I wish the fuck you would! You better remember I'm the one that be cooking 'round here, keep playing *with me* and you gone be shittin' so bad you gone lose weight!"

"Now I ain't eatin' shit else yo bald head ass cook. You got me fucked up. I'll make noodles every day just like I was doing before yo ass got here, fuck you mean!" Juice hissed back making me laugh harder.

"Boy fuck you, I'll throw all that shit away."

"You throw my noodles out you buying me some more

muhfucka!" The way he said it let me know that she had left the room and he was hollering after her. "On my soul, I'm gone fuck her ass up! What you said you wanted again bro?" He grumbled, finally addressing me again.

"I was tryna see if Dream was with y'all or at Destiny's crib. We were supposed to be talking and she got low on my ass." I managed to get myself together enough to say, only for him to start laughing.

"Oh damn, that's what the fuck you get nigga! It's about time she played yo dumb ass!" He guffawed.

"Nigga fuck you." I felt my face tighten in irritation. "How you making jokes about my shit and y'all over there fighting like y'all with the WWE and shit."

"At least my woman here and not somewhere running from me."

"Man is she there or not!" I growled tired of his lame ass jokes. Next time I saw him I was giving his ass a jaw shot, just for playing with me.

"Ahhhhh yo ass sound mad as hell nigga, tighten up!" His tone was teasing. "Nah but for real though Dream ain't over here. I don't think Destiny talked to her- you want me to ask?"

"Naw you know she wouldn't tell me shit no way." I shrugged defeated. I'd just have to catch her ass another day. She had to go home eventually, right? Busting a u-turn in the middle of the street I headed back towards my house.

"Damn you ain't bouta go cry is you? I told yo dumb ass to ask her about Budda before jumping to conclusions and shit. Now look at you." His laughter was the last thing I heard before I ended the call. I wasn't about to keep talking to his simple ass. As soon as we'd disconnected a call came through from Trell. I started not to even answer, but I did anyway just in case he had something important to tell me.

"Yooo."

"Nigga get yo ass to the club *now*!" He gritted into the phone

angrily before hanging up. Without a second thought, I maneu-
vered towards my club knowing that if Trell had told me to
come, it was something serious. I hadn't even been up there in a
minute, but the owner of the construction company, Mike had
the keys and knew what he was supposed to be doing, so I
figured that shit was running smooth in my absence. Trell's call
had me feeling like that wasn't the case, and I was more than
prepared to go fuck some shit up if Mike had been done
anything crazy in my shit.

I made it there a short time later, and as soon as I pulled
up, I recognized the unmarked car, which immediately put me
on high alert. I parked haphazardly and jumped out, saun-
tering over to the group of people standing in the club's doorway. Right away, I noticed the two detectives, one male and
one female looking completely out of place as they talked to
Trell.

"What's this about?" I asked cutting off their conversation as
I came to a stop beside Trell. I hated the police, and I definitely
hated detectives. They seemed like all they wanted to do was
lock niggas up and they were grimy enough to do so by any
means necessary. The one closest to me smirked at the sight of
me before reaching his hand out for a shake.

"I'm glad you could make it Mr. King." When I looked
between him and his hand in disgust, he quickly drew it back.
"We uh, ahem. I'm detective Jones, and this is my partner detective Brown. We'd just like to ask you some questions about Jeremiah. We were investigating the disappearance of a Dreon
Tayler, and his grandmother who was recently found dead was
under the impression that Jeremiah and Destiny Parker had
something to do with him being missing."

Without warning, I busted into a fit of laughter that had
them looking at each other in confusion. I couldn't believe
they'd brought their asses to my business to ask me this shit. It
couldn't have been protocol for them to come and question me

as opposed to the brother that was supposedly involved and even if it was it was stupid ass policing.

"Excuse me, but I don't think there's anything funny about an old lady being *murdered* in her own home, Mr. King!" The woman said, taking a step toward me angrily.

"Oh, I don't think that shit funny either. I was laughing at how stupid y'all look coming down here and pressing me about it. This the type of toy cop shit our tax dollars paying for?" Chuckling I looked at Trell who was already shaking his head as he held in a laugh himself.

"Shiiiit I guess so."

"You know what-!" She started, but I quickly cut her off, done with this bullshit for the day.

"Nah, let me get y'all fuckin cards. I'm gone have to have a long ass conversation with y'all boss 'cause this shit is unacceptable. Y'all muhfuckas down here questioning me about the next nigga grandma and still ain't found whoever it was that killed my OG!" I sneered glaring down at her. She instantly piped down, and her partner finally found his balls and stepped between us, pushing her back with a warning look.

"Go wait for me at the car Brown." He ordered. I watched as they stared at each other, having some type of silent conversation before she finally stormed off toward the car.

"Dammmn you gone be put on pussy punishment for that!" Trell cracked, making us both chuckle as detective Jones brought his attention back to us.

"His ass the one with the pussy, she bossed up way quicker than he did!" We shook up while he turned red from a mixture of embarrassment and anger.

"Y'all think y'all real funny huh? I wanna see how many jokes you're gonna have when you guys are sharing a jail cell."

"This nigga think he on *CSI:Miami* or some shit! Tryna kick them one-liners like you Horatio, nigga get yo bitch ass on!" Trell chortled, and we shared another laugh as dude walked away just as mad as his partner. Even though I was finding humor in the situation at the moment, I knew that they weren't about to let the shit slide. This was the worst possible time for the police to be sniffing around with Budda and Dre on the loose, wreaking havoc but them niggas were still going to die and if the detectives wanted in on it they could catch the same fate.

DESTINY

J'd been trapped at Juice's house for a week now, and we were already getting on each other's nerves. It was like he was intentionally trying to piss me off half the time, or it may have just been my hormones. When I was pregnant with Yo' Sahn I was the same way. My patience was short, and I was always ready to fight. Honestly, it was my regular attitude, but it seemed amplified while pregnant. As irritating as Juice had been since I'd met him, he was even more so now. He was on my ass constantly about what I ate and making sure I took those damn prenatal vitamins that often made me nauseous. It was to the point where I couldn't wait till he left the house every day just so he'd be out of my face. Yo'Sahn, on the other hand, had been feeling slightly neglected, since Juice and Eazy weren't taking him along like before. Add to that the fact that he was going through issues of his own from losing Ms. Rachel. My baby was moping around this house daily and I felt like there wasn't shit I could do about it. He was at the stage in life where he didn't want to hang out with me and Dream anymore, so most days that left him camped out in his bedroom playing the game, which was where he was now.

"What yo ass in here doing?" Juice came out of the bathroom looking like he was shooting a body wash commercial—six-pack on full display, with water glistening all over his body and steam following behind him. I sat up in the bed biting my lip as my pussy tingled just looking at him. Did I mention that pregnancy also made me horny as hell? Despite the arguing one thing we always did right was fuck and that was mostly because no matter how mad we were at each other sex always followed the argument. He dropped the towel that had been wrapped around his waist and whatever I was about to say got stuck in my throat. "Fuck you staring at me like that for?" He frowned when I still hadn't said anything.

"Come here." I half moaned whined tossing my hair over my shoulder as I scooted to the edge of the bed. This was one of the few times I wasn't wearing a lace front or a sew-in, and my natural thick hair was wild and free. Picking up on my vibe Juice's face fell into a smirk as he came to stand directly in front of me with that gorgeous dick hanging between us.

"Let me find out the only time yo evil ass wanna be nice is when some dick involved." Ignoring him, I continued to stroke his semi-hard erection before slowly easing my mouth down until I reached the base. That shut him up fast and I couldn't help but look up at him so that I could catch the look of ecstasy on his face. One of the things I'd learned while living there was that he was a sucker for some good head, and I always made sure to give him the best. I'd barely gotten started, and already he had his eyes closed and his mouth wide open. Turned on by how much he was enjoying it, I went even harder, mustering up as much saliva as I could and using my mouth like a vacuum. Moaning, I pulled away letting all my slob drip down his length, before swirling my tongue on his tip and gobbling it all back up.

"Sssssss, gahdamn Destiny!" he hissed, and it was my turn to smirk inwardly. A second later, he was pulling me away by my hair as he panted. I licked my lips and grinned up at him, enjoying the perturbed look on his face. "Take that shit off." He ordered talking about the silk, baby blue lounge set I was wearing.

"Lock the door first," I told him as I started to unbutton my shirt. Although, Yo'Sahn rarely came in the room without knocking, I didn't want to take the chance of him popping in and seeing me with my ass in the air. I quickly stripped while he sauntered over to the door and came back with his dick bobbing with each step. He made a flipping motion with his hand as he came closer, letting me know to get on my stomach, which was quickly becoming my favorite position these days. Happily, I laid down with my knees planted on the very edge of the bed and tooted my ass up for him. I was already soaking wet and ready, so the second that he ran his rough hand over my backside I quivered. Juice slid his dick up and down my center damn near making me come just from the friction alone, before inching his way inside of me.

"Ooooooh." I moaned as my pussy adjusted to his size, and he went deeper and deeper. My body tingled, and I put more of an arch in my back just like he liked it.

"Shut yo ass up, before shorty hears you!" he growled in my ear and grinded roughly sending a shiver down my spine.

"I caaaaan't, you're soooo deep." It felt like every nerve ending in my body was responding to him as he continued to pump in and out of me without mercy. With a low moan of his own, he buried his face into my neck and slowed down his pace, so that I was feeling every inch of him. That shit only made my cries louder, and he eventually placed his hand over my mouth to silence me.

"Fuuuck girl!" I'd pulled one of his fingers into my mouth and started sucking it like I'd done his dick just a few moments before. He was still delivering those slow and steady strokes, and as I felt my orgasm rising, I started throwing it back at him. My toes curled, and my stomach tightened.

"Ahhh, I- I'm cuuuuminnnng!" I cooed picking up my pace as my pussy clenched, and I exploded around him.

Grunting Juice slapped my ass and went harder, gripping both of my hips and slamming into me over and over again until his movements became jerky and I could feel him pulsing as he filled me with his seeds. We were breathing heavy, and I could feel his heart pounding against my back. "damn that pussy get better every fucking time! I'd have been got you pregnant if I had known yo shit would be this bomb!" he finally said planting a kiss on my shoulder and lifting off of me. Just that fast he'd ruined the moment with his rude ass mouth. Rolling my eyes I stood up, and walked right past his stupid ass headed to the bathroom.

"I'm surprised you could tell, you came so damn fast." I grumbled loud enough for him to hear instantly wiping the silly grin off his face.

"Fuck you just say?"

"You heard me nigga." I sped up just as I hit the bathroom door and tried to close it on him, but he pushed it back open.

With squinted eyes he stepped fully inside and towered over me. "stop actin like I won't fuck yo ass bowlegged girl." Again, I rolled my eyes, knowing that it would piss him off even more.

"I hope that wasn't a preview, cause if it was I'm highly disappointed." I teased trying to fight the laugh I felt bubbling up in my throat at the irritation that flashed across his face.

"I can't tell you was up in there moaning and groaning like a nigga was putting it down."

"So, you act like you ain't never heard of *faking it*. Slow ass boy." This time I couldn't stop myself from chuckling. "Ahh-!" my laughter quickly turned into a squeal as he scooped me up by my legs just as the doorbell rang. "you better go see what whoever that is want." That shit came right on time because for as much shit as I was talking he'd worn me out for real.

Nipping at my neck he didn't let me go. "the lil homie can

get it." He barely broke away long enough to say as he added some tongue and placed his already hard dick at my opening, getting me hot even though I didn't think I could go again. My body always had a mind of its own when Juice was involved though. He was dipping in and out of me with just the tip when there was a knock at the bedroom door. *Saved by the bell*, I thought as he grumbled but didn't put me down right away.

"Aye it's some police at the door!" Yo'Sahn said loudly, sounding like he was unsure. I felt Juice tense up at the mention of the police before setting me on my feet. We both rushed into the bedroom to throw on some clothes, and he quickly found his sweatpants from the night before and slipped them on. Once he was covered from the waist down, he swiftly walked out of the room while I was still trying to find my robe and draws. Thank God, Yo'Sahn had decided to follow him back to the door with his little nosy ass.

I gave up my search and settled for a pair of tights and a t-shirt, before racing out behind them. By the time I got to what I had thought was going to be a nasty scene, the two detectives from the police station were already beginning to walk away. Confused I slowed my pace and tried to think of what the fuck they could want as Jones looked back just in time to spot me over Juice's broad shoulders.

"Hey! I thought you said she wasn't here!" she shouted trying to make her way back to the door.

"So, call Smith if you wanna talk to us cause you ain't doing it without a lawyer. Now get yo funny lookin ass off my shit!" Without giving her a chance to reply he slammed the door in her face while Yo'Sahn stood by laughing and recording on his phone.

"What did they want?" A part of me was scared to ask since the last time I'd encountered them; they were questioning me about Dre. It seemed like even from the grave that nigga was causing me problems, and although I didn't have anything to do with his death that didn't mean I felt like being accused.

"Nothing important." Juice tried to dismiss my question as he hinted at Yo'Sahn whose face was now buried in his phone. "Aye, don't post that." He told him and I could already tell it was too late, just from the deer in headlights expression on his face.

"Uhhh… okay." His voice raised an octave even though Juice wasn't paying him any attention before he raced out of the room.

"So, you don't think its important that they're coming to your house looking for me while my son is here!" I pressed following Juice who was already heading back towards his bedroom. He ignored my question as he searched for his phone, finding it on the nightstand and sitting down on the edge pressing in a number. "You don't hear me!"

"Aye, Smith man them two detectives just left from over here. Why the fuck they coming to my crib and shit tryna question us?" his anger was evident as he listened intently to whatever Smith was saying, while I stood in the doorway trying to read into their conversation. I couldn't lie I was scared as hell. Asking questions about shit while I was in custody for something else was one thing, but for them to come here. It felt like they were really trying to pin this shit on us as opposed to just inquiring to rule us out. With everything I had going on I wasn't equipped to be doing prison time over Dre's trashy ass and I damn sure didn't want my baby daddy to either, regardless of if he was guilty or not. "Nigga I don't give a fuck! Keep them the fuck away from us, my girl's pregnant she doesn't need this stress right now!"

Despite the heaviness of the conversation, my heart pounded at his concern for me and our child. It made me feel a little bit safer knowing that he was trying to protect me from the police. That shit was new for me. Being with Dre and even Antonio I *never* felt secure, not from other bitches and definitely not from the shit they did in the streets. Without even having to be told I knew that it was going to be different with Juice. Not only because of his past actions, but also because of his present ones. He'd been there for me even before we got personal, and no matter how much he got on my nerves I couldn't deny that.

"Whatever man, set that shit up, but tell them not to approach us before or after!" he ended the call quickly then slammed the phone down beside him, and ran a hand over his curls with a grunt of frustration.

"What did he say?" I asked meekly coming fully into the room and kneeling in front of him. He'd dropped his head and had it resting it in his hands, but I lifted it forcing him to look at me.

"Dre's bitch ass grandma is dead, and since the shit happened after her name was brought up when they questioned you, they feel like that's more of a reason to press us. Smith said we gone have to go in and be questioned, he gone set it up, but don't even trip he gone be there the whole time ayite?" It looked like it hurt him to even have to say it, but what I was stuck on was the fact that Ms. Taylor was dead. Just like with Dre, something in his eyes told me that he had something to do with it and I wanted to slap the shit out of him. Once again, he'd placed me in a compromising position with his trigger-happy ass! No wonder he had seemed all concerned and shit, he knew that the reason they were sniffing around was because of him!

"Ughhhh you muthafucka!" without thinking I reared back and hit him across his jaw as hard as I could, catching him completely off guard. I hoped that I had knocked a tooth loose, but I knew that was only wishful thinking because he barely flinched. The only effect it had on him was his scowl deepening.

"Fuck you do that shit for!" he barked grabbing my arm as I tried to walk off. I snatched away but got in his face wearing the same angry expression as him.

"You know exactly why nigga!" I wasn't dumb enough to say

out loud what I knew, but it wasn't like I needed to anyway. He'd never admit it but who the fuck else would kill Ms. Taylor's old ass? Don't get me wrong she was rude and pretty much mean to everyone she encountered except her family, but nobody would have gone out of their way to kill her over it. Well, nobody except my baby daddy.

"Yo, you lucky you pregnant or I'd smack yo ass back-."

"I wish the fuck you would!" I spat. Juice knew damn well he wasn't gone hit me, pregnant or not. We both did.

"On my soul, I ain't bouta keep doin this with you. Yo ass can't be half in half out in this shit. You gotta know that sometimes shit gets messy fuckin with me, but I swear I ain't gone let shit happen to you, Yo'Sahn or this baby." He said placing his hand on my slight pudge as he looked at me intently. I searched his eyes for reassurance, but the truth was I didn't really need to. I trusted him to do exactly what he said every time, and he was right, I couldn't continue to be one foot out the door with him if our shit was going to work. "You with me?"

Sighing heavily I gave him a quick nod. "Yeah, I'm with you." Relief washed over his face as he wrapped me up in a tight hug. No doubt in an effort to further comfort me, but that wasn't necessary. Although I was still a little scared, I knew that Juice was going to make sure that I was good just like he said. Besides if he didn't and I ended up going to jail or some shit, I'd kill his ass myself.

BUDDA

I'd finally set up the meeting with Santos, and I was hoping that our extensive history would make him take pity on me. Not only did I need soldiers, but I needed guns, and a front on the work tip. I made it to his family's restaurant with ten minutes to spare, and I took that time to get myself together and do a couple of lines.

"Nigga you wanna do that shit *now?*" Dre questioned looking at me crazy. He'd been acting real funny lately after not having the money to bury granny, but that was his broke ass fault. The old bitch barely fucked with me like that, so I didn't care one way or another, but I knew that her death would work in my favor to get him to do some crazy shit. Things weren't going the way that I thought they would. I'd been hoping that by now I would've already gotten my bitch back and been living the life that was stolen from me, but apparently not. I was starting to feel like this was karma coming to bite me in the ass, yet I still held out hope that Santos would help. His assistance would at least get my foot in the door.

"So, don't worry about me and what the fuck I got going on."

I warned, smudging my middle finger on the glass tray to pick up the remaining residue and rubbing it on my gums. Since he knew better than to fuck with me, he shut his ass mouth and threw his hands up in surrender.

"Just sayin'."

"Yeah, well don't just say shit! Now when we get in here let me do all the talkin, Santos don't know you, so he probably won't even let you come into the back anyway." I didn't even give him a chance to respond before I was climbing out of the car. Spanish music blasted loudly from the two-story brick building as we walked up and the smell of tortillas met us at the door. Santos' son, Manuel was coming out of the back as we entered looking just as disgusted by my presence as always. His fat ass had never liked me, and I felt the same way. He was lucky to have been born into wealth and his position while niggas like myself had to get it out the mud and work under him. For as long as I'd known Santos, his son had been a bitch, using his father's name for clout but had the nerve to look down his nose at me.

When him and the two goons that were with him reached us, they wasted no time checking us for weapons while Manuel watched with a sneer. "Hey *Manny*." I teased knowing that he didn't like when I called him that.

"Don't call me that shit nigga!" he spat as they finished searching us with a quick nod. "I don't know why Santos fucks with you, but I definitely don't trust you *rato* (rat)!" I knew better than to try Manuel in here, but I would remember his disrespect for sure. It wasn't like he brought any value to his father's organization so if his ass died one of these days I was sure that Santos would assume he'd just crossed the wrong person, but he wouldn't suspect me. Even though I was fuming inside I managed a tight-lipped smirk as I passed him and went to the back where Santos was waiting. They instantly stopped Dre though forcing him into a booth up front.

"Budda!"

When I entered the small room that he used as an office, Santos was sitting behind the desk, but he stood as soon as he saw me.

"What's up Santos, long time no see." We shared an embrace before both taking our seats with smiles. Things were getting off to a good start, I mean at least he was happy to see me, right?

"Yeah, I know. I heard you'd gotten out, but I've been tied up. You know these young muhfuckas out here stay in some shit that fucks up business." I could see the irritation on his face as he talked about it, and I knew exactly what he meant.

"Man these new niggas is knuckle heads." I said shaking my head in fake concern. "But that's why I wanted to come talk to you. I'm sure you hear of Eazy and Juice they're the main ones bringing in these young niggas and letting them run wild."

Squinting, he tilted his head in confusion. "Yeah, I'm aware of them, they're my boy's competition but what that got to do with anything?"

"I'm glad you asked. I think me and you should take them totally out the equation. Think about it, if we get rid of them and take over their territory, then we'll have dominated a huge part of the city. We could be kings of this shit-!"

"Brian." He said my name slowly, lifting both hands. "I hear you man, but I can't get involved in a plan to take them down."

"What! You scared or some shit!"

"I'm scared of no one *hijo de puta*!" He fumed, jumping out of his seat. "Those boys are protected by *Pierre*! Do you even know who that is! There won't be a fight it will just be death, and I'll take the biggest hit on my end, so no I don't want to involve myself in this!" I couldn't believe that he was acting like this. Like a scared little bitch. It seemed like Dre had more heart than he did, but that was cool. If he didn't want in on this plan then I'd just do it without him and then take over his shit when I did.

"Ayite, cool Santos. But when I do this shit and come out on top, don't be trying to come get on the winning team!" I didn't miss the disappointment in his eyes as I stormed out, but at this point it was fuck Santos. I would get what I had coming to me by any means!

DREAM

"*E*azy got some damn nerve! Why you ain't call me?" Destiny asked after I'd filled her in on the other day's events. We'd just dropped Yo'Sahn off at school and were on our way to breakfast so that we could figure out our next move. Although, I'yanna had basically told me we were shit out of luck as far as rebuilding, I wasn't going to let that deter us. Ms. Rachel wouldn't have wanted that and I knew that she hadn't expected for the insurance to play us this way. I really missed that lady for real. No one had ever looked out for us the way she had, and I was sure no one ever would.

I immediately shook my head. "You know damn well if he didn't find me at home yo spot would've been the first place he went to look."

"True." She agreed rolling her eyes with an aggravated groan. "Juice told me he was looking for you when he called the other day, and I ain't think nothin of it cause we was already arguing and shit."

"Well, I ended up going to our mama house anyway-."

"Whaaat! How did that shit turn out?" She gasped, wide eyed.

"You already know it was a mess. She started talkin shit about the salon and blah blah blah. Same ole same ole." Sighing, I pulled into a parking spot in IHOP's lot as I thought about how bad things had gotten that day. I'd never wanted to slap my mama so bad, and she had said some evil things to us, but that day she'd been extremely insensitive in addition to my already fucked up mood. It was just a recipe for disaster.

"That shit crazy. Girl, what's wrong with yo mama?" She tisked shaking her head as she took off her seatbelt and grabbed her wallet from the center console.

"She yo mama too hoe!" I shot back.

"And she was yours first, so what you saying." She gave me a pointed look before shrugging and getting out.

"I swear I can't stand you." I chuckled meeting her outside of the car. "Maybe yo rude ass will simmer down after you feed my lil niece." I playfully rubbed her stomach, and she swatted my hand away with a growl as we walked into the building.

"Niece my ass! I bet not be pregnant with a girl." Surprised by how adamant she was about not having a girl, my expression must have given away my confusion, prompting her to suck her teeth. "What?"

"Why don't you want a girl? I would've thought with Yoshi and Juice's aggy ass you'd want another female around to even things out." Shrugging, I let my voice trail off because the look on her face was one of horror.

"Hell naw! Can you imagine another me! I ain't even ready for that, nope. Give me another boy all day, then Juice can take them both outside with him!" She quickly dismissed, and we both fell out laughing as the waitress finally walked up.

"Well when you put it that way." I agreed.

"Is it just yall two?" the waitress interrupted with her nose turned up as she rolled her eyes. It was clear that she had an attitude, and I wasn't sure from what, but she wasn't going to take it out on us.

"Ugh, I don't like your attitude. Can we get another waitress please-?" I squinted down at her name tag. "Olivia." A closer look at her face displayed the fading marks of a black eye and bruising, and I instantly felt sorry for her, even though she still had a stank demeanor. The muscles in her face grew tighter at my request, and without responding, she walked off, sucking her teeth in irritation.

"Bitch I will-!" Destiny went after her, and I quickly snatched her back.

"Aht aht, I don't think so bitch." I instantly shut her mean ass down. I could tell that she'd been around Juice's ass a whole lot lately because she was even more evil than usual. I could only imagine how his offspring would be.

"Girrrrl, she itchin' for me to give her ass another black eye, she tried it with that shitty ass cover-up. That's probably why she really mad!" I was trying my hardest not to laugh at her ignorant ass, but it was definitely a lost cause. She was still stewing as what appeared to be a manager came over smiling brightly, and holding two menus.

"Hello ladies, I'm sorry for any issues. My name is Jessica, and I'll be handling your meal for today." She said before leading us to a booth table not far from the door. "Can I get you anything to drink?"

"Pepsi please."

"And I'll take orange juice. Thank you." Destiny added with her head buried in the menu. Jessica quickly jotted down our drink orders and went to fetch them while we both figured out what we wanted to eat. I always perused over the different options every time we came here and ultimately ended up ordering the same thing pancakes, cheese eggs and bacon. By the time Jessica returned and placed our drinks on the table, I already knew that's what I wanted, and I quickly put it in. Destiny on the other hand was being extra as fuck.

"Okay, let me get the crepes with strawberries, eggs scrambled light, bacon and an order of sausage links."

"You gone eat all that?" I asked and she nodded vigorously.

"Yep, Juice been tryna make me eat extra healthy shit since I been at his house. This the first time I've been able to sneak away and eat what I want." She seemed extremely satisfied about being able to eat her super sugary and greasy food too. "Look this probably his aggravating ass right here."

I giggled inwardly. Despite how I felt about his rude ass, I couldn't deny how he'd been there for my sister, and it was cute that he was checking up on her. That thought was quickly dismissed as I watched her face turn from mildly aggravated to straight angry.

"What! I'm on my way right now! Yall bet not let them near my baby!" Destiny fumed jumping up from the table and tossing out some bills. "Bitch we gotta go back to Yo'Sahn's school! Antonio's bitch ass actually called DCFS!" Without asking any more questions, I grabbed up my purse and followed her out the door. It was definitely about to be some shit if they tried to take my nephew over that nigga's word!

When we made it back to the school, I didn't even park straight before we were both hopping out and making our way into the building. As soon as we stepped foot in the office the secretary jumped straight up from her desk and in front of Destiny, trying to stop our advancement.

"Where the fuck my son at Sheron!" Destiny shouted still charging forward and inevitably making Sheron back pedal.

"T-they're in the office, but you can't go back there!" Her voice raised an octave as Destiny damn near shoved her out of the way and stormed into the principal's office, slamming the door hard as hell. Sheron was still picking herself up off of the floor when I walked past and entered the office behind Destiny to see Yo'Sahn sitting in the office with the principal and another lady that was clearly from the state.

"Yo'Sahn get up, we're going home!" As soon as his mama gave the order he did as she said looking extremely relieved.

"Ma'am, I'm-." the woman tried to speak finally gaining Destiny's attention since she'd been focused on Yo'Sahn who was grabbing has bag.

"I don't want to hear shit you got to say lady! I don't know you and my son damn sure don't know you, so I should have gotten a call in regards to any conversation involving him!" Destiny shot a glare towards the principal who was literally shaking in her seat. When her eyes landed on me looking for back up since she knew I was more rational, I held my hands up. I was only there to get my nephew and make sure that my sister didn't get locked up, which was quickly looking like a mission I was going to fail since the caseworker kept trying to talk to her.

"I don't need to get your permission to talk to a child that may be getting neglected ma'am. You can come in here yelling all you want, but unless you want him taken away then I suggest you allow me to finish my interview peacefully."

"Do you even hear how you sound? Does this boy look neglected to you! He doesn't miss not one meal, he ain't getting beat on and his grades are better than half the kids in this school! You have no basis to interview him about anything!" she fumed moving within arm's reach of the lady. I immediately pulled her back slightly, because she already had gotten arrested for assaulting Dre's grandma. If she hit this lady they for damn sure would lock her ass right back up.

"Then you have nothing to worry about correct?" the lady said tilting her head smartly. "I assure you honey, I've been in worse situations than this. Now, I don't necessarily believe that there has been any wrong doings from what I've seen so far, but I still need to make a report. I'm asking that you allow me to do so, so that you and Yo'Sahn can return to your day." As much as I could see that Destiny wanted to keep arguing with her, she managed to control herself long enough to release an angry gust of air and a slight nod.

"Fine," she hissed turning to Yo'Sahn who was visibly upset. "Go head Yoshi, I'm gone be right here when you done." Without speaking, she pointed back to the chair he'd been in when he tried to protest, and he plopped back down sulking.

"Thank you." Instead of answering her, Destiny exited the room behind me, making sure to slam the door after herself. Grumbling she quickly made a phone call to who I assumed was Juice until she started cursing up a storm and I realized she'd called Antonio. After tearing him a new asshole on his voicemail, she hung up and paced the small area, talking shit under her breath. This shit was about to open up a whole new can of worms. Any hope I'd had for Antonio had been washed away that fast and I prayed he got his shit together before Juice found him although we may have already been past that.

JUICE

I was ready to kill Destiny's bitch ass baby daddy after finding out what he did, but I was already being watched by the police while they did this fuck ass investigation so I had to let him be. When she'd told me what had happened at the school and why I was fuming. The whole time I'd known their asses, I'd never seen that nigga and now all of a sudden, he wanted to try and take Yo'Sahn away. I was pissed off even more when she told me that he'd come up to the hospital trying to speak on my presence in shorty life, when he hadn't even been there. That nigga was begging for me to come see him, but I needed to clear me and Destiny's names first.

Today was the day that we had to meet with the detectives and no matter how much I tried to reassure her, Destiny was nervous as hell. I squeezed her hand before bringing it to my lips as we pulled up in front of the police station.

"You cool, cause we can do this shit another day if you want." I asked dead serious. If she told me that she wanted to go home, then I'd pull clean off and tell Smith to pick another day. She was already going through a bunch of shit, and this was only adding stress to the situation. Sighing she shook her head and looked up at the building with her lip turned up.

"Nah, we might as well get it over with." She shrugged not knowing how sexy her strength was to me. I always bragged on what type of mother she was and how she got shit done, because I loved how strong she was. All this time I'd been chasing pretty ass bird brained bitches, but Destiny had brains and beauty. She was nothing like any of the hoes I'd had in the past, in fact, she was reminding me of my OG more and more.

"Ayite cool, here come Smith now." I spotted him a few cars ahead making his way towards us in an expensive ass suit like we were going to court or some shit. Destiny had tried to dress up too, and I shut her straight down. Wasn't no way I was gone let her walk up in there in a pencil skirt, trying to suffocate my baby. I snatched her up some joggers just like I was wearing and a t-shirt. There was no telling how long they'd be trying to question us, and I wanted her to be comfortable, and warm since it was always cold as fuck in them interrogation rooms.

We both stepped out at the same time and met him on the curb, as he grinned widely showing all thirty-two teeth at Destiny. I swear he wanted me to go across his shit.

"As always, it's a pleasure seeing you Destiny." He simpered, reaching for her hand, and I quickly grabbed it up in my own, intertwining my fingers with hers.

"You keep trying me Smith, and I'm gone break your shit." I told him causing his grin to drop completely from his face. He straightened his tie and cleared his throat uncomfortably, but I hoped that he'd heed my warning. That flirting shit was probably cute to his other clients, but I didn't play that shit.

"Sorry." Taking a step back he put his focus on me making sure not to even look Destiny's way. "I talked to both detective Jones and detective Brown, and told them that I'll be sitting in on both interrogations. So, one of you will be waiting while the other is questioned if that's okay with you." his question was directed at me, but Destiny was the one that spoke up.

"Wait, waiting in here?" her displeasure was evident on her face as she pointed up at the building.

"You can go first and I'll wait, and you can just leave when you done." I wasn't pressed about being there. Regardless of what they thought they had which I knew to only be the coincidence of Ms. Taylor dying after her report. That wasn't shit to me, I hadn't left any evidence, and I hadn't told Destiny shit about what I'd done, so they had less than nothing. Nodding she accepted my offer to go first mumbling an okay.

I walked in with her and Smith giving her a quick kiss before they were escorted away by one of the lazy ass police that sat behind the desk. As soon as they disappeared around the corner, I dipped back to the car. Wasn't no way I was going to be sitting in there with all of them staring at me all crazy and shit. I wanted to flame up, but I wasn't stupid enough to do it right outside of the police station, so instead, I grabbed one of the edible rice crispy treats I had stashed.

Thirty minutes later I'd swallowed three more and was listening to J. Cole's latest joint high as fuck. I had my seat laid damn near all the way back and my hat pulled down over my eyes dozing off when my phone rang. I really ain't want to answer that shit, but with the way things were going I couldn't afford to.

Seeing that it was Eazy, I didn't hesitate to answer. "What's up bruh?"

"Shit just made it down to the club, I was just making sure yall was cool. I know you had to do that thing today." He said referring to us being questioned by the detectives. When he'd told me about them coming to the club and harassing him I was highly irritated. It wasn't like it was out of the norm for them to stalk a nigga whole family, but I didn't see the point. If anything they were damaging their own case on some goofy shit, and I had to wonder who had allowed them to become detectives in the first place.

"We just got here not too long ago. Smith and Destiny went in first though, since she all nervous and shit." I let him know, absentmindedly looking out at the cars driving past.

"Them muhfuckas ain't got shit, she gone be cool."

"I already know, I done told her slow ass, but you know her and Dream ain't used to this type of shit." I sighed and ran a hand down my face. If they were just wanting me then I wouldn't even care because I know how they do, but since they were coming after Destiny too it was different. Especially since she was pregnant. Behind my child though, I'd blow this whole precinct up, so it was in their best interest not to stress her out.

"Facts, but let me call you back bruh these fuckin construction niggas don't know what the fuck they doin!" Before I could even respond, his rude ass had already hung up. He was a bitch for that but I was too high to even trip. Besides that, I was getting restless as hell just sitting in the car waiting. Realizing that I hadn't talked to my pops in a few days I dialed his number hoping to check up on him. He hadn't been himself since my Og passed, but he'd been hanging in there. Shit the first couple days I ain't even want to eat, but Destiny was on my ass. That just reminded me of what he was missing, not having his back bone there. After all this shit died down, I'd have to make sure that I looked out, because we were all he had anymore.

"What yo ass want Jeremiah!" he huffed as soon as he answered.

"Man yo old ass sound just like Eazy." I chuckled sucking my teeth. "I'm just tryna see how you doin and you talkin crazy."

"Maybe I sound like him cause you get on both our nerves lil nigga." He joined in my laughter, and it felt good to hear him not sounding as down as he had the last few times we'd talked. "I'm cool though man, watching some game highlights and drinking a beer."

"That's what's up. I was gone come see you and bring Yo'Sahn with me after I take care of this lil business."

"Uhhh, sounds like a plan, just-just call when you on the way." I didn't miss the hesitation in his voice, but I wasn't going to let that stop me from going to see him.

"Bet, I might can get Eazy to bring his ass too…..hold up this him right here." I accepted Eazy's call putting us on three-way. "Aye pops on the line bro-."

Boom! Boom! Rattattatatat!

Gunfire erupted through the phone, instantly stopping my heart. "Eazy! Aye Eazy!" Me and my pops continued to yell his name as grunting filled our ears.

"Elijah! Jeremiah if this a joke this shit ain't funny nigga!" my pops went off.

"It ain't! I'm on my way to him now!" I barked jumping in the driver's seat. Tossing the phone I pulled off, weaving in and out of traffic cursing out loud as I realized I'd left my gun at home. This was not the time for this shit! I can't even lie, tears were stinging my eyes as I defied the speed limit trying to get to my brother. Horns were blowing and people were cursing me out from the grand theft auto type of driving that I was doing and I nearly got into at least three accidents by the time I actually made it to his club. I slammed the car in park and jumped out, running into the building ready for whatever gun or no gun and damn near dropped to my knees at the sight of the massacre on the first floor. It looked like at least twenty construction workers scattered across the floor and covered in blood. They obviously hadn't been expecting whatever had gone down.

"ELIJAH!" I shouted his name as I made my way through the bodies and to the stairs, that led to his office. The longer I went without hearing anything the more my heart pounded in my chest. "ELIJ-ah, fuck bro!" my voice cracked as soon as I made it to his door and saw him sprawled out on the floor next to his desk, with his shirt drenched in blood. Rushing to his side, I lifted him into my arms as the tears I'd been trying to hold on to finally spilled out across his face.

"Ju-Juice," blood gushed from his mouth as he struggled to speak, looking at me with wide terror-stricken eyes.

"Don't try and talk man, I got you. Stay with me bro ayite, stay with me." I could barely get out anything coherent between being overwhelmed with emotion and trying to search for my phone. I quickly realized that I'd left it in the car and angrily clenched my teeth so hard I thought they'd break. Frantically, I searched for his phone or at the very least his office phone so I could dial 911, and my eyes fell on another body in the room. Further inspection revealed that it was Dre. Half of his face was blown off and covered in blood, but there was no mistaking who it was. I knew right then that he'd come in busting and Eazy had delivered him a fatal shot after taking multiple rounds. Even though that nigga was clearly dead I still wanted to pick up the AK he had lying beside him, and shoot until his head was completely gone, but getting Eazy to the hospital was more important. It was hard to tear my eyes away from his scum ass, but I managed to, and a second later I found the phone lying right up under the desk. After calling 911 and alerting them of what happened, I continued to talk to my brother, even as his breathing grew more hollow and shaky. Then I did some shit I hadn't done since I was a little ass kid…..I prayed.

An hour later, I was still praying as we waited in the emergency room for a doctor to come and tell us something. My pops was slumped over in a chair in the corner with his face buried in his hands, and I knew it was to hide his tears. Once again he was trying to be strong, but I knew that shit was hard on him. Destiny had called shortly after we'd gotten there and ended up telling me she was done with her interview, but I'd forgotten all about that shit. I told Smith to tell them fuck ass detectives that I would reschedule when I could because my focus was on my brother at the moment, and I didn't give a fuck how they felt about it. I tried to get him to give Destiny a ride home, but she'd insisted on coming, so she sat next to my dad trying to comfort him even though I knew she was fucked up too. In addition to what she had to deal with earlier, I'm sure this situation was like déjà vu to her. She met my eyes and gave me a reassuring smile, but I wasn't even in the headspace to return it. I needed to know something, and I was damn near ready to take off to the back myself. Releasing a long and irritated sigh, I finally took a seat and tried to get my emotions under control, but the shit wasn't working. My eyes landed on the door, and was surprised to see a face I wasn't expecting. He walked right over to where we were and I stood up to meet him.

"Pierre, what you doin up here?" I asked confused about seeing our connect. As far as we both knew he stayed out in New York, so it was weird to see him there. In all the years we'd worked with him, he only came down when it was time for a meeting. Pierre didn't even come up for shipments so this shit was throwing me for a loop.

"I was in the area and heard about what happened to Elijah, so I stopped by. Is there anything I can do or get to help?" that shit had me squinting at him suspiciously but when my pop's head shot up and hate filled his face, I knew it was about to be some shit.

"What the fuck are you doing here nigga!" He roared shrugging Destiny's hand away and jumping in Pierre's face.

"What you think Elijah? Rachel's dead now, ain't no more lying about the shit!"

I looked back and forth between the two as they faced off, trying to figure out what the fuck was going on. How they even knew each other was beyond me?

"Nigga don't speak my wife's name!" my pops thundered.

"I know one of yall better tell me what the fuck going on!"

they just continued to stare each other down without speaking while I waited growing more and more pissed off.

"You gone tell him or you want me to?" Pierre questioned barely moving his lips as he spoke. This entire time he seemed more composed than my pops and the more he talked, the angrier my old man got. Before he could answer the doctor came out and called for family members to step forward. For the moment the conversation was paused, but as soon as I got word on my brother we were going to get to the bottom of this shit.

"Well, Elijah is strong. He suffered a total of six wounds three in the abdomen, one in the leg and two through and through in the arm. He did suffer a collapsed lung, but we were able to stabilize him. Now he will need a blood transfusion, is anybody willing to be tested?" the doctor said matter of factly, looking at each of us.

"No need to test, I'm his father." Pierre said shocking us all.

BUDDA

I still had yet to hear back from Dre, after I'd sent him on that dummy mission earlier, but that had been the point. My hope was that his slow ass would go in and get himself killed more than anything at this point. I was tired of supporting his bum ass! He was more of a drain than anything, and if what I had planned was going to work, then I needed to limit the people involved. Did I want to kill Juice and Eazy? Hell yeah, but them niggas had nine lives or some shit, and it was way harder to find anybody to get on my team than I thought it would be. At this point I was a one-man army, besides Olivia and I planned to use her ass too if I could.

"What are we doin here Budda damn!" Olivia whined from the passenger seat irritating me instantly.

"Don't ask me no fuckin questions! We gone do what I say when I say it!" as soon as I raised my voice, she winced only infuriating me more. She was acting as if I hadn't walked her through this entire thing already, but that was the way she tweaked. Yeah, you read that right she was snorting coke and lacing blunts right along with me now. After that last ass whooping, I'd put on her she'd let me get her hooked on the very drug she claimed to despise. Us getting put out after I'd tricked off the rent money, helped in making her depend on it even more. Her being addicted personally helped me have even more control over her, but at the same time, it made her jumpy as fuck, which often pissed me off. The plan had been to send Dre off to try and kill Eazy, and while they were distracted killing or torturing him, Olivia and I would rob Trell after he did his pick-ups. It would be one of the easiest licks I'd ever hit, and it was literally idiot-proof, which is why I didn't mind having her with me. Two heads are better than one, even if one of them was lacking common sense. Besides, I needed a driver while I did the snatch and grab. I didn't trust that her stupid ass wouldn't fuck something up then I'd surely have to kill her,

and I really didn't want to do that just yet. If it wasn't for her constant yapping, I would've never run into Trell in the first place. One of the many nights that I'd taken her car and gone out on the hunt for more drugs I'd peeped him leaving the known trap with a duffle bag. I played it cool and followed him back to his house. It took a week of me following him around for me to get his schedule down and when I did I realized that he was doing the pickups for Juice and Eazy. That opened up a whole new possibility for me, I could literally kill two birds with one stone. If I stole their money, I could fuck them up and get back on since Santos had no intentions of loaning me shit.

So, now we were sitting almost a block away from the trap, waiting on Trell to come out with the last bag of the day. I figured I might as well do it big and snatch up everything I could at once. Not too long later, I saw him bopping down the front steps, and I quickly tapped Olivia on the arm. "Aye, follow that car." Of course, she couldn't do so without rolling her eyes and smacking those fat ass lips. I had to restrain myself from smashing her face through the window, because I knew if I did, she wouldn't be able to drive anymore. Weak ass bitch would probably pass out, then I'd be on my own, and I couldn't afford that.

"Just do what the fuck I said!" I barked forcing her to jerk out into the street. "Bitch, I swear if you fuck this up for me, I'm gone beat yo ass! Now go!" I was damn near foaming at the mouth dealing with this silly bitch, but thankfully she got her shit together and began following him from a safe distance. After all of this time, I knew that he was headed to his house to do the count and then he'd take the money to Juice like he was his little bitch or something. So, the closer we got to his place I had Olivia speed up. "go, go, go!"

She pressed the gas harder and pulled up alongside him with fear and anxiety covering her face. That didn't stop me from jerking the wheel towards his car and slamming right into the side of it.

"Ahhhh what the fuck Budda!" She shrieked loudly, clutching her face like the kid from Home Alone. Still holding onto the wheel, myself I pulled my gun out.

"Put yo gah damn hands back stupid!" I spat turning my attention back to where Trell was attempting to get away. He seemed like he was struggling to pull out his own weapon and I wasn't about to let him shoot me. As soon as I knew that Olivia had control of the wheel, I fired three rounds out of the open window, instantly shattering the glass on his car and hitting him in the neck. His car fishtailed and veered right off the road, and I pointed for her to follow. By the time her dumb ass finally pulled over, and I got out I could see Trell trying to crawl away. The look on his face when he saw me was priceless, but not more than what he had in his trunk. Without thinking I raised my gun and shot him in the back of the head dropping him right on the grassy hill, he'd made it too. After making sure he was dead I grabbed each of the six bags and place them in her car, before jumping back in.

"Get us up outta here now!" she was pulling off before I'd

barely had the words out of my mouth, but it was necessary because it was already people out trying to pull over and help. Little did they know that nigga was dead and he wasn't comin back........

TO BE CONTINUED.............

TEXT TO JOIN

To stay up to date on new releases, plus get exclusive information on contests, sneak peeks, and more...

Text ColeHartSig to (855)231-5230

Made in the USA
Middletown, DE
16 March 2021